Allur

Naomi Schmitt

MaxQ Enterprises, L.L.C.
Printed and bound in the United States
Cover design by Amanda Pankonin
Sketches & map by Naomi Schmitt
Cover photo by Linda Lee
ISBN: 978-1-939894-00-7
$21.95

✝ Prologue ✝

Baldemor stood before a beautiful lake full of clear, shimmering water. Moments before he arrived, it had been a grey, decaying meadow. No animals had been present in a long time, and with none of the wildlife carrying seeds, from plants and flowers they brushed into or ate, there was no fertilizer for the grass. Because of this, the lake eventually filled up with dirt, and the grass began to whither. Upon walking onto this once beautiful land and seeing death, Baldemor conjured his powers and made a crater in the midst of the decaying grass and filled it with fresh, crisp water. Already, a doe with her young fawn had come to drink.

He stood silent, starring at the picturesque scenery he had created. His mind focused on the thoughts of his future, the future of the human woman he loved and their child, who was yet to be born, and the future of this realm.

"Do I really want to lose all this power?" he thought to himself. He knew the answer, but it put a heavy chain around his heart.

He thought back to the day he met Raleigh, how he

instantly fell in love with her. It happened one day as Baldemor was traveling and came upon an Abbey. As he neared the wall that surrounded it, a woman was just leaving. She was so alluring the sudden feeling caused him to stop and say hello.

The woman was on her way to get a cart for a crate of books she just received from her brother. Baldemor was so mesmerized by this human female that he offered to carry the books to the cart for her and then escort her home. She blushed and accepted his offer. How could one refuse the charm of a god?

When they had arrived at her cottage, she asked him to stay for dinner as a thank you. They talked while they ate. Baldemor decided he did not want to leave. Now, Baldemor's time on Earth was nearly up—he could already feel his powers being pulled from him.

The gods were only allowed to walk on Earth for short periods of time. If they stayed longer, they would lose their godly powers and become mortal. This curse, as it seemed to be, was put upon all gods by the Ruling Gods, the oldest and wisest of all of them.

So would he give up his powers to stay with Raleigh and their child, or go back to his realm and continue his responsibilities? If he stayed, Xandor would become the High God of War and all would fall into chaos. Xandor despised the humans. He saw them as slaves—toys for him to play with. Baldemor truly cared for the human race. That was why the Ruling Gods chose him to be High God of War in the first place!

Now, as Baldemor stood at his lake, he thought deeply about the situation he had gotten himself into. He realized his real question was, *"Do I live a mortal life and be with the woman I love, raising our child in a world full of fire and bloodshed at the hands of Xandor, or leave and let the child live the life she was destined, in a world where I can ensure that war will not harm her?"* He knew what he had to do, even if it made his heart ache.

Baldemor returned to his beloved and explained the circumstances to her. Raleigh already knew that, as a god, his time on Earth was limited, but the pain felt fresh and there was another problem.

Back in his realm, there was an extremely jealous goddess who thought Baldemor belonged to her. It had been an eternity since Baldemor had expressed romantic feelings toward this goddess, but she insisted they were still life-long partners. For Raleigh's safety, and the child's, it would be best if they were apart. He could not bear it if something happened to one of them and if it happened to both, he didn't think he could live with that. So to ensure that the goddess could not harm them both, he pleaded that Raleigh find a family to raise the child.

And thus began the fate of the child they would have; half-god, half-mortal—a demi-god.

† Chapter One †

"How do you like your birthday present Jerriney?" asked her aunt Tesa.

"I love it!" Jerriney said as she ran outside to whack the weeds in the backyard.

It was Jerriney's seventh birthday, and she had just received her first wooden play sword.

"I told you she would like it," John whispered to Tesa.

"Are you sure it's a good idea though? It won't make her grow up to be a violent girl, will it?"

"I'm sure it will be fine. We will teach her that it is not used against other people, only trees and wooden dummies," John assured her.

"Alright, but if she starts hitting the village kids with it I want you to take it away." There was a knock on the door. John went to answer it.

"Hello!" John said as he cheerfully opened the door. Once he saw who it was, a concerned look washed the joyful expression off his face. "Oh, come right in. Tesa, the king's messenger is here," he said over his shoulder.

"What do you want?" Tesa asked a bit harshly.

"The king is in need of your service. He asked me to send you on your way this very day. I am to take Jerriney to a new couple. I believe you know them," the man said.

"Who is this couple?" John asked.

"Ron and Elizibeth Drouger."

"Yes, we know them well. What does the king need of us?" Tesa asked.

"He did not fill me in with any details. Just that it was very important and that you must prepare for the worst, for you may not come back alive."

"We cannot leave!" Tesa burst, "She's only seven, and we cannot leave her if there's a chance we may not come back."

"The king is in dire need of yo—"

"We cannot leave her!" Tesa interrupted the messenger. "I know I am not really her mother, but she is very dear to me." She started crying for she knew they could not disobey the king.

"Tesa, we cannot stay here. It is the king's orders. If we disobey him we may be banned from his kingdom, or worse, executed. He may just take us out of his service since we are close to him, but we need to serve our king. We signed for life."

"I know, but I did not know we would come to have Jerriney. I want to stay with her. Could just John go?" She was speaking to the messenger now.

"No. The king specifically said both John *and* Tesa. I have orders to not return without the both of you. Now collect the things you wish to take, and that does not include the girl. I will take her to the Drougers when you two leave. Go now and may you have god-speed."

So John and Tesa told Jerriney what was happening. After they said their goodbyes, they packed some rations and a couple changes of clothes as well as their weapons. Then they gave Jerriney to the messenger and went to the stables to ready their horses.

"You ready Tesa?"

"No. I wish we didn't have to go. I have a feeling we will never see Jerriney again."

"I wish we could stay too. I wish we could raise her and live as a happy family, but we swore an oath to the king before we received Jerriney. Let's go Tesa. The sooner we get this over with the sooner we will get home and see Jerriney again." They mounted their horses and left for the king's palace in Morga.

The king's messenger took Jerriney to a nearby inn while they waited for James to arrive. James was another messenger of the king's. Every time John and Tesa had to go on a mission, James would take Jerriney to her temporary family, but he was busy with family matters when the king needed the message sent, so a different man delivered the message.

Jerriney had lived off and on with John and Tesa ever since she could remember. Because they worked for the king she often found herself with a family that watched over her while they were on a mission. James always made sure the new family could properly take care of her. Jerriney had found a place in his heart. Once, he even took her home to his own family.

James and Jerriney walked side by side, something they had done quite often. *"So why does today seem different?"* Jerriney thought as they meandered through the streets of Ascillia. *"I know why I'm going to a new house, but James seems worried, like something bad has happened, or will happen. It's not like we haven't been through this before. I wonder why he hasn't told me anything yet. He always tells me before we leave the house. What could be wrong?"*

At that moment, James looked down. He noticed her staring at him with those eyes. He looked away. To him, her face showed signs of frustration. *"Or is it something else, maybe anger?"* he thought.

In all his years of working for the king not once had he seen a human with such strange and alluring eyes as Jerriney's. They were green, like an emerald, and they shined—almost glowed when she got excited. What amazed him was that she had no pupils in her eyes.

James finally broke the silence, "Jerriney, your aunt and uncle are going to cross the ocean for their mission this time. The couple I'm taking you to are close friends of John and Tesa. We don't know how long they will be gone. It might be longer than you are used to."

She was silent.

"Do you understand Jerriney?"

She nodded at him, moving her gaze to her feet.

The Drouger's house was a little ways out of the city, close to the edge of the forest. James was admiring the scenery when he noticed the house was up ahead, so he nervously looked down again. She was still staring at him but with curiosity, not frustration like before. He smiled as they finally arrived at Jerriney's new house.

"Here we are Jerri." He knocked on the door loudly. The blast to the door rocked the frame, and made Jerriney slightly nervous.

Suddenly the door opened and revealed a young and handsome looking man. Jerriney figured he was either in his late twenties or early thirties. She had always enjoyed guessing the age of people she met and found she was usually correct. It had become sort-of a game for her. Since she saw many people when she moved from house to house, she found it enjoyable to test her knowledge and try to guess peoples age along with other things such as their job or hobbies. Sometimes she was able to get to know the person and see if her guesses were correct. She decided that this man looked like he was thirty-one.

"Hello? Oh hello! Is this Jerriney?" said the man looking from Jerriney then to James. "Did I say your name right?" he asked rather quietly. He didn't want to offend his new ward.

"Yes, you did," Jerriney replied timidly.

Enthusiastically, the man invited them in. Jerriney noticed him beaming, but she was more interested in the house. Jerriney scanned the inside, her eyes instantly finding the windows. One was in the kitchen above the sink and another in the living area to the left of the door. Two chairs were placed in front of the window in the living area, angled as if to frame it. A couch was up against the wall on the left side, facing the fireplace opposite to it. A table was the only thing indicating the end of the living room and the beginning of the kitchen. On the table was a single candle emanating the only light in the house. There was a fireplace, but it was empty; the couple had doused it, waiting for the light of the new day. The floor was polished wood planks. Glancing right, she saw a small hallway which, she figured, led to sleeping rooms. Inside the kitchen was a woman with her back to them. Jerriney was about to survey the kitchen, but her observation was cut short.

"Liz and I are so very excited to meet you Jerriney!" said Ron.

Jerriney nodded, but made no reply.

James spoke on her behalf, "Thank you for volunteering to care for her on such short notice Ron."

"Of course! It's not a problem. Liz and I are happy to have her!" James looked at Jerriney, to see if she was excited, but she was still looking at Ron.

James kneeled to Jerriney's level as he spoke to her, "Jerriney, this is Ron, and Elizibeth is there in the kitchen. They are your new caretakers. Your aunt and uncle are good friends with them, so there is no need to be worried or afraid."

"I'm not afraid of anything!" She knew he was just looking out for her, but she wanted to seem big and smart to this man that he had called Ron, so her remark came out a bit harsher than she had originally hoped. She bit her lip thinking they would be offended, but was glad to see them both laughing.

"I'm sure you're not. We have been told by your aunt and uncle that you are very brave. We know quite a bit about you from them," Ron stated as he lovingly patted her on the head.

"I'm not a dog," she blurted quietly, looking at the floor. Ron looked at James who merely shrugged his shoulders signifying that he was just as baffled as Ron.

"Oh, well I'll be sure not to do that again, and I'll remind Liz that we do not have a dog in the house." Ron winked at Jerriney. "Well, why don't you two make yourselves comfortable while I go check on breakfast?" He gestured toward the couch.

"Actually Ron, I'm needed back at the palace. I think I might take my leave now," James said as he stood up and turned to Jerriney. "Jerriney, will you be all right if I return to the palace?"

Jerriney was looking about with curiosity. "Yes, of course I will. I'm seven. I'm a big girl. You just run along back to your king," she said waving him off.

18

With that, Ron escorted James to the door. "She sure acts mature for seven." He seemed confused by this.

"Yes, well, she is exceptionally smart for her age, but do not let that fool you! She can be a handful at times." James left on that note.

After James was gone, Jerriney sat on the couch and waited patiently for Ron to come back with Liz. After a few minutes Ron and Liz came out of the kitchen.

"Jerriney, this is Elizibeth," Ron stated. Liz looked at Jerriney curiously and then finally she realized why she was having trouble looking away from her. It was her features themselves. They were all stunningly beautiful. Her eyes were the color of emerald gems and her hair was white as snow; it slightly shimmered silver in the light of the rising sun coming through the window. What stunned her most was the fact that beautiful didn't even describe her. It was more than that; she was more than beautiful.

Shaking off her expression she said, "Hello Jerriney. You can call me Liz."

"Hullo Liz." Jerriney looked her over with

scrutiny. Liz was tall, had satiny black hair, and was very charming, perhaps twenty-nine. That was as far as she got in her assessment of her new mother figure before Ron interrupted her thoughts.

"Well, Jerriney, would you like to see your room?"

"Yes please," she humbly replied.

Ron started down the hallway. "Follow me."

"I'll go and finish breakfast. I hope you like your room Jerriney." Liz called after them as she walked to the kitchen.

Ron led her to the room they had prepared for her to sleep in.

"It's not that big, but when you get older we can build you something bigger."

"This will do for now. As you said, I will need a larger room when I am bigger." She walked around her new room. She seemed to have more confidence now.

"I made a cedar chest for you. It's sitting out in the barn. It should only be about two or three days until I have completed it. Oh! We have some toys you may like. We kept them from our childhood."

"Alright. I shall look at your toys. Do you have a forest nearby?" She looked at Ron with her unusual emerald eyes. It was then he realized she had no pupils. *"How does she see?"* he wondered.

"Uh yea, just out the back door. We have a large forest as our backyard. There are many furry creatures too, if you like animals."

"I love animals!" she burst. He noticed that her eyes had a certain luster to them. That was the first time he recognized excitement in her. He did not expect such a reaction. After they talked for a while he showed her where things were in the house. Then he left her in the room to put her own things where she wanted them.

This was Jerriney's favorite part of moving to a different house—the new things she was given, and an unexplored environment in which she could have new, never before imagined adventures.

When Liz was done cooking she called Ron and Jerriney to the table. She set the table with the food and let Jerriney eat a bit before they spoke.

"Would you like us to call you Jerriney or do you have a nickname?" Liz asked her.

"You can call me Jerri. That's what I am usually called," she replied between bites of oatmeal.

"Alright Jerri," Liz said trying out the new name. "Do you need more food?"

"No. Thank you. This was a very delicious meal." Jerriney smiled. "I think I'll like it here."

Liz beamed at the young girl's response.

They had a taken in a foster child once, but it was a boy and he was extremely troublesome. They almost lost half their house when he decided to start his bedding on fire. She was glad Jerriney was a girl. After breakfast, they sat around the fireplace while Jerri told them about herself and what she liked. They asked if she needed anything more for her room, but she said it was fine for now and that if she needed anything she would let them know.

Jerriney settled in with Ron and Liz quickly. It was almost as if she had known them before she came to live with them. She rarely quarreled with them and always ate her vegetables, on the rare occasions they had dessert they let her have seconds if she ate everything on her dinner plate. She still missed her aunt and uncle, but living here was not miserable.

Years passed, and Jerriney began to grow into a beautiful young lady. She helped around the house and was even helpful to Ron, cutting firewood and getting deer meat ready for winter storage. She spent a lot of her time in the woods. She seemed one with nature and often took in injured animals or ones that had lost their parents. As she grew, her interest in sword fighting and archery grew as well. More years went by and she became seventeen. Now, she had mastered the bow and arrow, but she had yet to go out on a hunt. Ron promised he would take her someday soon.

† Chapter Two †

Ten Years Later

One bright and cheerful morning, the sun had just come up, the birds were chirping, and Jerriney was going on her first official hunt with Ron. Before, she did not like the idea of killing animals herself, but if Ron became sick there would be no one to provide food for the family. She loved animals, but her adopted family came first. Hunting became less malevolent as long as she hunted for food rather than pleasure. She never took a doe or a baby deer. She once made Ron hunt only bucks. But she soon realized that if they hunted only bucks then eventually there would be none left in the area and the deer would not be able to reproduce, so she let Ron hunt female deer if he made sure it had no young or was pregnant.

Now that she was seventeen Ron said she was almost ready to go by herself. Before she hunted on her own though, he wanted to show her the best spots and other things she should know about hunting as well as other creatures that may be a threat to her.

"You go ahead and wait for me on the porch," Ron

24

said. "I'll be right there."

"What!? You said right after breakfast. It's twenty minutes after breakfast! Can't you wait to do whatever you have to do until we get home?" Jerriney complained.

"I'll be right back. I just have to, visit the privy."

"Oh." Jerriney blushed.

"Jerri, where are you?" Elizibeth shouted.

"I'm out here on the porch!"

"There you are! I've been looking all over for you." Liz handed her a water skin. "Drink plenty of water so you don't get dehydrated. And stay out of Ron's way. I don't want you coming home with an arrow in your thigh."

Jerriney smiled. "Liz, I'm seventeen. I think I know to get out of the way when someone is pointing a strung bow at me. Anyway, I will do the hunting today. Ron is just showing me the best places to find deer."

"Oh honey, I know. I just can't believe you're seventeen already," Liz said. "It seems just like yesterday you were running around my feet making me almost trip."

"Ready Jerri?" Ron asked as he walked out of the house and joined them.

"Ready as I'll ever be."

"Okay, let's go!"

"Be careful!" Liz said as she waved goodbye.

After they had gone a ways and were out of sight of the house, Ron stopped. "I didn't really go to the privy."

"What do you mean?" This confused Jerriney because Ron never lied. "What did you do then?"

Ron had a huge smile on his face. "I got you something." Jerri then realized that his hands had been behind his back. He brought them in front of him along with a beautiful short bow. "This is for you. It has never been used. I've been working on it while you were out in the forest. It's sort-of a memorial, if you will, for your first hunt. It's made of Elvish wood. You've grown up to be a fine young woman. I'm sure you will be an extraordinary huntress."

Jerriney took the bow. "It's beautiful." Her eyes sparkled with intensity like they did when she was excited. "Thank you!" She hugged him. "How did you get Elvish wood?"

"It was actually a gift from your aunt and uncle. They brought it back from one of their missions for the king and gave it to me knowing how much I like to craft things out of wood."

"Ah, I see." There was a moment of silence.

"I can teach you how to make your own some day, in case you lose it or you want to make one for someone else." They smiled at each other.

"That sounds nice." Jerriney put the bow on her back. They continued on into the forest.

𝕿𝖍𝖊𝖞 got home just in time for supper. While they ate, Ron and Jerriney talked about their hunt. When they were finished, Liz looked at Jerriney and said, "Jerriney, remember when you first came here when your aunt and uncle went to work for the king?"

"Yea. Why?" Jerriney did not like discussing such things because it reminded her that she may never see them again.

"I have some bad news." Liz paused to gather the dishes. "While you two were away hunting, James stopped by. He said John and Tesa had died on their way home." She wiped away a tear forming in the corner of her eye. "They were traveling by boat and were ambushed. No one survived except the ship's captain."

Jerriney looked at the table and said nothing. Her

face grew grave. "How can they know for sure? Did they find the bodies?"

"No, they didn't find any bodies. All they found were pieces of the ship floating on the water. Only the captain survived, as I said before," Liz answered.

Jerriney made a mental note of that. She planned to speak to this captain. Something sounded wrong about the whole situation.

"Did James give you any more details?" Jerriney asked.

"No that was all that he said. I asked him if he had more to tell, but he said that was all he knew," Liz quietly said.

"Why did only the captain survive?" Jerriney wondered. *"Aren't captains supposed to go down with their ship? Don't they consider their ship their life?"* She was now *very* determined to find this captain.

"Did James give the captain's name?" she asked.

"No, he didn't, but before John and Tesa left they gave James something." Liz took the dirty dishes into the kitchen and brought back a small pouch. "In case they did not return he was to send it to you." She handed Jerriney the pouch.

"It's full of blue stones. Do you know what they are for?" Puzzled, Jerriney took one out and handed it to Ron.

"I don't know. James just said they were from John and Tesa. He didn't say anything about what was inside," Liz said.

"You should take them to Loreen. She might know what they are for," Ron suggested as he rolled the stone between his fingers.

Loreen was, well, Loreen! People went to her with farm trouble, animal trouble, health trouble, pretty much anything they needed help with. She knew the ways and writings of old. You could never anticipate what she was going to say or do and no one knew her actual age. She looked to be in her mid-sixties, but she would have to be at least one-hundred to know the ways of the old!

Jerriney often went to visit her. She enjoyed learning new things from her and found the old woman to be quite humorous. So the next morning Jerriney went to see Loreen.

† Chapter Three †

"Come in!" Loreen said. "Oh hello Jerriney! Haven't seen you in a while! How are you?"

"I'm fine, thank you," Jerriney replied.

"Just fine? Not splendid or fantastic? Just fine?" Loreen questioned.

"Well, I just found out my aunt and uncle died in an ambush. They sent me this pouch full of blue stones, which is why I came to see you. So yes, just fine."

"Oh." Loreen paused and glanced out the window, as if expecting to see their ghosts looking over Jerriney. "I'm sorry to hear that. Good friends of mine John and Tesa were. They were so curious, never stopped asking questions. It's a shame they don't get to see you now, but enough chitchat! Let's see those rocks!" Loreen quickly changed the subject so that neither of them would start weeping.

Jerriney handed the pouch to Loreen. Loreen took it and walked over to a table piled with old papers and poured the stones out onto the table.

"Pretty blue rocks they are. Let's see—one, two,

three, four, and five! I'll need some time to look at these and I'll also need to go pull out some old books. Come back in a week and I'll see what I can tell you." Loreen smiled at Jerriney and abruptly opened the door for her. Jerriney thanked the lady as she left.

On her way home she thought about how strange Loreen acted. Normally she would offer tea and cake and chat a while, but this time she seemed eager to get Jerriney out.

"She must know something she doesn't want to tell me yet," Jerriney thought.

When Jerriney reached the porch a large, black housecat jumped in front of her.

"Where have you been?" Jerriney asked as she stroked his smooth fur.

"Out." His voice resonated through her head. She did not understand how he spoke to her in this way, but she had grown accustomed to it. Loreen had given him to her, so she assumed that he was some kind of magical cat.

"Out where, Nerezzan?"

"In the woods."

"What were you doing?" Jerriney tried.

"Walking."

"Whatever, Nerezzan." She pressed him no further

as she knew how stubborn he could be. She also was eager to share how her meeting with Loreen went. "I went to see Loreen today. She's going to find out what those blue stones are for."

"For looking at, I presume," the black feline sarcastically said.

Jerriney glared at Nerezzan and went inside.

"How did it go?" Liz asked.

"Good. She had me leave the stones there and told me to come back in a week."

"That probably means she thinks they are important," Liz said. "How are you feeling since learning about John and Tesa?" She looked at her, concerned.

"Well, I don't really remember them since I was only seven, but I do feel sadness. I wish I could see them now. I could actually talk with them since I am older. It would be nice if they could see how much I've grown."

Liz hugged her and said, "I'm sure they would be very proud of you."

𝔗hat night, Jerriney spent most of her time in the woods talking with Nerezzan and even sparring with dead trees. She asked Ron if he would spar with her, but Liz insisted that it was too dangerous.

When she arrived back home, Ron mentioned that their meat supply was getting low and asked Jerriney if she could replenish it while she was waiting on Loreen. She left the next morning.

Since she had a week, she decided to spend the night in the forest and hunt the next day. It had been a while since she had relaxed and just listened to the sound of nature. When the sun went down, she decided to study the stars. She spoke to Nerezzan while they gazed at the night sky.

"I wonder if the stones actually mean something," Jerriney said to him. "I wonder if because of them I will get to go on an adventure like John and Tesa did."

"Oh you'll go on a far more dangerous adventure than your aunt and uncle."

"What do you mean? How do you know that?"

Nerezzan just licked his paw and said, *"I know many things."*

Jerriney pondered on that for a while. *"I've heard myths and legends of creatures called Werecats living hundreds of years and knowing things before they happen. I wonder if that's what Nerezzan is and what exactly he knows. If he knows anything about the stones he probably won't tell me until after I've spoken with Loreen again, but I'll try."*

"Nerezzan, what do those stones have to do with me?"

Nerezzan was quiet.

"Please tell me," Jerriney pleaded.

"I will aid you when the time is right."

Jerriney wished to question him further and try to get answers out of him, but she knew he was in one of his stubborn moods and would get nothing more out of him. She decided to call it a night and question him when he was in a more willing mood.

𝔍erriney spent the next two days hunting. She was still learning, but Ron had taught her all he could and said the rest she needed to learn by personal experience. On the second day she finally found tracks leading to a nesting place. By what Ron had told her, she knew there was a good chance they might come back to this spot, so she hid in some bushes. It wasn't long before a juvenile buck sauntered into the clearing. It seemed as if he had fallen behind the rest of the herd and came here looking for them. Jerriney swiftly strung her arrow and shot true.

She was glad she wasn't far from where she made camp. Although this buck was young, he was still quite heavy for her. Since she knew she could not carry a buck all the way home on her own, Jerriney brought along a cured bear hide that had holes along the edges so she could put a rope through it. She laid out the hide and rolled the deer on it. Jerriney then pulled the ends of the hide together and put the rope through the holes. In this fashion, she hauled her catch home after she packed up camp. When they got there, Nerezzan went inside and curled up by the fire while Jerriney took care of the deer.

"You're just in time for supper Jerri. Come and sit," Liz said as Jerriney walked through the door. "Ron will be late. He had some business in Ascillia to take care of." She set the table for two. "So how was your hunt?"

"I caught a young buck. I put it in the meat house for Ron to skin 'n stuff when he gets back."

"Great! Make sure you tell him, so it doesn't go bad. What else did you do while you were in the forest?"

"I talked with Nerezzan. I think he knows something about the stones." Jerriney took a bite of corn.

"Well I wouldn't be surprised! We all know he is some kind of magical creature," Liz blankly stated as she sat down.

"He didn't even tell me what he knew! He just said that he'd tell me when the time is right. And lately he's been talking in riddles and not telling me what they mean," Jerriney continued. She looked over at the cat, frustration crossed her brow.

"At least he talks to you. I can't even get a 'good morning' or 'hello' out of him," said Liz as she buttered a piece of bread.

"I can't understand him anymore and it frustrates me when he doesn't tell me what he means."

"If I were you I would stop pestering him and wait until he decides to tell you."

"Okay," Jerriney said defeated.

For the rest of that week, Jerriney busied herself by helping Ron get her deer ready for storage and went on another hunting trip bringing back two small does.

When the morning of the day that marked a week arrived, Jerriney quickly got ready to see Loreen. She was headed for the door when Liz stopped her.

"Aren't you going to eat breakfast?"

"I'm going to see Loreen," Jerriney cheerfully said.

"Oh yes, I almost forgot, about that, Loreen

stopped by before you woke and said she was going to Kale today and that you should see her tomorrow."

"Oh. Alright," Jerriney replied, slightly disappointed.

"But Ron wants to talk to you," Liz said. "He's in the meat house."

"Okay, I'll eat first." Jerriney sat down at the table as Liz gave her a plate of scrambled eggs.

She hurriedly ate her breakfast then went to the meat house. Ron was just finishing skinning the two deer she had caught the day before.

"Mighty fine deer you caught here." Ron beamed. "It will make good meals."

"Thanks!" This made Jerriney happier as not being able to see Loreen dampened her mood. "Liz said you wanted to see me."

"Yup. Come on, let's go find a clearing in the woods."

They quietly walked through the woods for a while until Ron stopped and said, "This will work."

They had arrived in a fairly large clearing.

"What are we going to do?" Jerriney inquired.

37

Ron didn't answer. Instead, he pulled out two swords.

"Nerezzan tells me you've been fighting trees. He says you're ready for something new, something more challenging." Ron handed Jerriney her sword.

Jerriney's eyes grew wide and started to sparkle as she took her sword. "Really? What will Liz say?" She paused for a moment then said, "How did you get Nerezzan to talk to you?"

"Liz and I already discussed it, she is fine with it. As for Nerezzan, he's been talking to me since those blue stones came. I think he knows what they are."

"Did he tell you?"

"No. He said I was not a part of it yet, whatever that means. Now, get your sword out. We'll go slow at first."

For the rest of the day, Ron taught Jerriney the basic techniques for fighting with a sword. Jerriney learned very quickly. They sparred until lunch time then they started walking home.

"What do you think Nerezzan meant by you're not a part yet?" Jerriney asked Ron.

"I haven't a clue. All he told me was that I needed to train you in fighting and defending. You already know how to use a bow so we just need to work on

38

your sword skills."

"I can't wait to see Loreen tomorrow," Jerriney excitedly said.

𝕷oreen knocked on a big, embellished, mahogany door.

"Hello?" A male voice answered. "Oh Loreen! It's good to see you!" They embraced in a warm hug. "Finally came out of that little shack of yours I see! What brings you here?"

The man was her brother, Neal, whom she had not seen in many years. He lived in a big sumptuous house. He even had a room big enough for a small museum that was full of books, old and new. This was the reason for Loreen's coming.

"Well I came to see you of course! There's no one else to see in this house except that mutt of yours and the butler!" Loreen lightly fibbed.

"Now, now, she's not a mutt. She's a very special breed of which she is the last of her kind."

"Alright, fine." Loreen rolled her eyes. "That elegant dog of yours. Is that better?"

"Much." Neal chuckled.

"Well are you going to invite me in or are we going to stand in the doorway all day?"

"Oh yes! Do come in! Would you like some tea? And maybe a little cake?"

"Yes I think that would be nice," Loreen said as she stepped through the door.

"Splendid! You may go on to the library while I get the refreshments. You still know where it is, right?" Neal teased.

"Of course! I couldn't forget a thing like that!" So Loreen hobbled her way past a few doors, mostly closed, turned a few corners and finally came across two large, red oak doors, similar to the door outside.

She smiled. Yes, she remembered this place. Her father made it for his only children, Neal and Loreen. It was still full of all the old books she remembered, which was a lot, and also with a couple more shelves of newer books. There were several tables and even more cushioned chairs around so you could read in comfort. There was a small living room area near the back, complete with a fireplace. She found a table for them to sit at in the right corner at the back of the room. She started browsing the shelves, got out a couple books here and there, then sat down and waited for her brother.

"So how's it going in Ascillia?" Neal asked his sister as he set the tray down.

Loreen took a sip of hot tea and took a plate with cake on it. "Good. Nice little town. More of a village these days."

"The name Ascillia just sounds like a big city like Morga."

Morga was the biggest city in Amensdale. The king's palace was built there on a hill. The town was built around it. Outside the city walls, there were a few small communities that considered themselves part of Morga, but those that lived in the immense city thought the opposite of these poor people.

"It used to be the second biggest next to Morga, until those wraiths came and destroyed most of the city. That's why the name sounds like it doesn't fit the small town," Loreen said then took a bite of her cake.

There was a pause as the two sat in silence while they recalled the events that occurred twenty years ago.

Big lizard like people appeared in Amensdale. The town's people started to call them wraiths because they wore black cloaks and seemed to float. They first showed up in Gurda Valley, which is just outside of Ascillia. They eventually migrated into the mountains or were killed by frightened people.

"Oh yes, I remember that dark time. That's when the people started building stronger houses, but now they've mostly forgot those foul creatures." Neal took a sip of his tea. "I see you've picked out a few books." He examined her quite tall stack.

"The Mordellian Prophecies?" Neal picked up the book. "What do you want with this? The writings in here have all been regarded as foppery."

"I thought I'd brush up on my prophecy stories; whether they're true or not doesn't matter."

"But *The Mordellian Prophecies*? Why not choose something peaceful that doesn't speak of death and torture so much? You want it for something else don't you?" Neal looked at her skeptically.

"Oh, alright. A villager in Ascillia brought me some stones so I came here to get some books that I remember have the description of them. None of the books in my library have the information I need, but I remembered there were a few books in here that spoke of them."

"So you didn't come to see me." Neal lifted his eyebrows playfully.

"No! I wanted to see you too!" Loreen exclaimed, not wanting to hurt her brother's feelings.

Neal looked at her skeptically.

"Oh fine. You caught me. I just needed some books. Mine don't have the stones I'm looking for in them." Neal handed Loreen the book.

"Alright, well." He started looking around on the shelves. "What are the stones that you're looking for called?"

"Promotheans."

"Promotheans? Are you sure?"

"Yes, the blue kind."

"Hmm. Whoever brought you those rocks are in for a lot of adventure."

"Yes, I know. I need to find out what exactly I'm dealing with."

"Well let's see, ah! Here we are, Promodic Legends and Prophecies. That and those other books you have there should help you."

"Yes, thank you," Loreen said humbly.

"No problem! That's what families are for!" Neal put the book on her pile.

"I should be leaving now. There's a sale on herbs here in Kale I wanted to get to before I left. Do you mind if I take a few books with me?" Loreen asked as finished her tea.

"Of course, take as many as you need. You can

even borrow my cart if you need it." Loreen smiled and looked over her selections again.

"I don't think I'll need a cart. Since you pulled out that book with Promodic legends, I don't think I'll need all of these." She picked up what she wanted and they walked back to the door.

"Oh, yes! Before you leave, what happened to that magical cat of yours, um, what was his name?"

"Nerezzan."

"Yes, Nerezzan. Do you still have him?"

"No, I gave him to a friend."

"I see. Well he might know a little something about those rocks. He was around during the time they were used."

"Yes, I forgot about that. I shall indeed have a little chitchat with him. Well, farewell, my brother."

"Goodbye Loreen and good luck!"

✝ Chapter Four ✝

A month after the ambush, that took Jerriney's aunt and uncle, a young boy walked into the king's throne room.

"The captain is here, sir."

"Good! Send him to the private lounge," The king replied.

"Yes sir."

When the king walked into the large lounge a middle-aged man was sitting patiently in a scarlet colored recliner. He had a sea-faring look about him. His face was shaven clean and his hair was dark blonde—longer than normal but not yet touching his shoulders. It was combed back nicely. He had dressed appropriately for a meeting with the king.

When the man noticed the king had entered he stood up and bowed.

"No need for that captain. This is a casual meeting."

"Sorry, my lord." He sat back down once the king had settled into his chair. "How has your day been?"

"Oh, good so far. There is not much going on right now except for the planning of the ceremony for all the people that were lost on that boat. I lost three of my best men and women that day, two of which were coming back to see their adopted child. It was her birthday when I took them away from her. Poor child." The king looked sadly into the fire as if he was watching the boat sink.

"That was a fateful day. I do not know why I was the only survivor. I only wish John and Tesa had survived. Either that or I had died with them," the captain replied.

"Now don't say that. If you had not lived, no one would be here to tell what happened." The king removed his gaze from the fire and looked at the man. "I will order one of my servants to find the best ship builder and have him make you a better boat. No not a boat, but a bigger vessel. One of those new fancy ships for you."

"Thank you, my king, but I'm sure I can get myself another one."

"No, no, you deserve it. After all, not only did you lose your vessel but you lost many men too."

"True. I will accept your offer, but do let me pay part of the cost," the captain pleaded.

"Nay, it will be a gift. I will take care of the expenses. I have not invested my money on such a great project in a while. It will be my pleasure." The king smiled.

"Very well sir. I will not press the matter any further for you are the king."

"Wise choice." The king chuckled. "Let us discuss why you came here. I need to know exactly what happened that day."

"Of course, where to start? I think I'll begin a couple minutes before the ambush."

"They came out of nowhere," Captain Dashlegar Crainten told the king, "those vile goblins on evil sea serpents. They were first seen in the North. We were traveling east at the time. A young boy, the lookout, spotted them first. Before he could say anything one of the goblins shot him in the heart with and arrow. Then they came at us faster. When they reached the ship I yelled, 'abandon ship!' but your people were too loyal and tried to fight back. I jumped off the side opposite to where the goblins boarded and I waited a while in one of the rowboats, but no one came.

"After it was clear I was the only one choosing not to fight, so I left. I watched my boat go down and the goblins return to their mounts. One, he seemed to be in charge for he kept yelling at the others and was also much larger, looked me right in the eye and grinned an awful grin. I thought he would shoot me with his bow but it seemed he wanted me to live in guilt thinking that I, the captain of that boat, should have done something to help. But I didn't. I fled like a coward and for that I lost my boat, my men, and I failed you my king." Dashlegar wiped a tear with his handkerchief.

"It was not your fault. You could have done nothing but fight and go down with all the others. Then I would not know what happened to my men. And now we know of these, goblins you say? I thought we drove them all out." The king put his elbow on the arm of his chair and rested his head on his fist.

"I know there was nothing I could have done. A captain always goes down with his boat, but not me," Dashlegar replied, seeming to ignore the king's comment about the goblins.

"Time heals all wounds." The king rose from his seat. "Or so they say." He gestured towards the door. Dashlegar got up and followed the king out.

If someone were secretly watching them they would have seen Dashlegar smirk as if he had just done something horrible and felt very good about it.

Jerriney decided to stay out in the woods the night she had sparred with Ron, for the stars were shining ever so brightly. Ron sent her off with plenty of meat she could cook over a fire and Liz told her to take Nerezzan in case something happened or she needed help.

Jerriney and Nerezzan were gazing at the stars and talking, like they so often did.

"The stars sometimes tell the future, or the past," Nerezzan said.

"Do they say anything tonight?" Jerriney curiously asked.

"They say many things tonight for a great deal of things have come to pass."

"Will you tell me anything?"

"There is a legend of old that tells about the coming of a horrible man, barely human, and the stars say it is finally coming true."

"So you mean the horrible man is coming?" Jerriney was a little worried now.

"Yes. I do believe the stars tell the truth and I sense it in my soul. You must keep a good watch out for signs."

"What signs?" Now Jerriney was a little scared.

"You will know when the time comes. You should not be so worried, but he has already started and taken down a boat."

"You mean the one my aunt and uncle were on?"

"Yes."

"So it wasn't a real ambush. He purposely killed them. Does that mean he purposely let the captain survive?"

"Yes. He set the ambush up, but your aunt and uncle might still be alive."

"You mean he didn't kill them?" Now Jerriney was confused.

"There is a possibility that they survived."

"So I might see them again? I might live with them instead of Ron and Liz?" Jerriney wasn't sure if she wanted to leave Ron and Elizabeth. She was full of questions.

"Yes! Would you stop interrogating me? You will find the answers to all your questions in due time. As for now, I've already said too much."

"Oh I'm sorry." She blushed. "I shouldn't have asked so many. I'm just really curious and excited."

"But you mustn't tell Liz or Ron yet."

"Okay." There was a short pause and Jerriney was hesitant to question Nerezzan any further for fear of angering him but she finally came out.

"Why not?" she asked

"Because it is not the right time or place. Now that's enough talk for now. You must get some sleep."

"Yea, I am pretty tired." Jerriney rolled out some blankets and put one in a pile near her pillow for Nerezzan.

"Good night Zan." The cat purred. She had not called him Zan in a long time.

"Good night Little One."

51

Jerriney was soon fast asleep and dreaming of reuniting with John and Tesa.

✝ Chapter Five ✝

Nerezzan was the first one up. He stretched and went for a walk. He got back just before Jerriney awoke.

"Good morning Nerezzan."

"Good morning."

"Curses! I forgot to pack something for breakfast. All I have is a little bit of leftover meat from last night." Jerriney riffled through her pack, searching again for food other than meat.

"I found a berry bush not far from here. They are big, juicy berries and they are ripe."

"Okay. Lead me to them."

Nerezzan led her to the berries and Jerriney picked enough for herself, but Nerezzan said he preferred the meat so they went back to their camp.

"Do you want me to cook the meat for you Nerezzan?" Jerriney asked.

"No thank you. I'll eat it raw."

"Alright," Jerriney shrugged and threw him the meat.

"Thank you." Nerezzan began eating.

When they were done with their breakfast Jerriney packed up their stuff and decided to go hunting.

"Ron said I could try and catch more deer while I'm out to help start getting the stock ready for winter. We still have a couple months, but he wanted to try out this new compartment he made that he thinks will keep the meat longer. I think now is a good time to hunt. Would you like to tag along?" she asked Nerezzan.

"I think I'll rest here in the sun. Don't be gone for too long," was all that he said.

Jerriney found some deer prints that led to what looked like the place where some deer had spent the night. She found some fresh prints that led the opposite direction so she followed them and soon spotted a young buck lagging behind. She took aim. The deer was grazing on some grass. She loosed the arrow. Perfect! She went to get the deer when she saw something sparkle in the dirt.

It was a blue stone. It looked just like the ones she had been given by John and Tesa but this one had silver tendrils in it that seemed to be swirling about, but Jerriney wasn't sure. She pocketed it and then went to the deer. She wrapped it up with her bear hide and picked up the rope to drag it back to Nerezzan.

When she got back, Nerezzan told her to quickly pack up her stuff and that they needed to go.

"Why are you in such a hurry?" Jerriney asked him.

"No time for questions, just go."

So they started home. It was soundless and daunting on the way back.

𝔍errine𝔶 walked through the door. All was quiet. "Hello? I caught another deer. I left it in the meat house. Is anybody home?"

Someone rushed down the stairs.

"Jerriney! Thank God you're back!" Ron seemed a little overly anxious to see her.

"I was only gone for one night." She set her pack by the door. "You knew where I was."

"I know, but come with me." Ron led her up the stairs to his and Liz's room.

Liz was lying on the bed asleep.

"What's wrong with her?" Jerriney looked at her pale face.

"The town healer doesn't know. She said she's never seen or heard of the symptoms."

"What are they?" Jerriney asked, almost afraid to

ask.

"It started at lunch yesterday right after you left. She suddenly passed out. When she woke I made her some soup but she felt full so she didn't eat it. She didn't eat supper either. Then she started coughing up blood and fainting a lot. So I went and brought back the healer. She said there was a better healer in Duvok, but Liz is too weak to be moved and the healer is afraid the journey would kill her, so I sent a messenger to get him but it will take a good four days to get there depending on the weather. Kathandra, that was the healer's name, does not know how long Liz has got. Loreen also came over and gave her some plant I didn't recognize. She said it would lower the fever and settle her stomach so she could eat." Ron sat on the bed next to Liz.

Jerriney noticed his hair was disheveled and she could tell from his eyes that he was up all night worrying about Liz.

Ron pushed some fallen hair out of Liz's face. "Loreen said you should stay with Liz and see her some other time."

Jerriney sat in a chair next to the bed. Nerezzan came in and jumped on her lap.

"This is why you wanted me to hurry wasn't it." Jerriney stroked Nerezzan's fur.

"Yes," he purred.

Jerriney started crying. Ron moved to another chair on the opposite side of the bed and quietly wept.

ℭ𝔥𝔞𝔱 next morning Jerriney woke in her bed with Nerezzan by her feet. Ron had carried her to her room when she started dozing off so that she wouldn't be sore in the morning. She sat up and Nerezzan crawled onto her lap.

"Do you know if Liz is going to die?" she asked him.

"I do know," he replied.

"Are you going to tell me?"

"No."

"I suppose it's best I don't know anyway."

She got up, put Nerezzan down and went to see Liz. Ron was feeding her soup.

"How is she?"

"She's awake, so I guess that's a good sign. The weather has been quite nice so it should take less time for the messenger to get to Duvok. He'll probably get there half a day earlier which means the doctor should be here earlier too, if he decides to come. I hope Liz can last that long."

"Why wouldn't the doctor come?" Jerriney had a quizzical look on her face.

"For a number of reasons," Ron replied as he worriedly scratched the back of his head. "He might be busy with patients of his own or he might already be helping someone in a different town. He might even not care about the people in our small village and just ignore our plea."

"Oh." Jerriney looked at the floor for a while then returned her gaze to Ron and asked, "Can Liz talk?"

"I think she hears because she has grunted and made small noises, but she hasn't spoken yet. Her mind must be occupied with whatever ails her. She also nods her head and her eyelids flutter once in a while. She's swallowing the soup so I guess the herb Loreen gave her works. Hopefully that's a good sign."

Ron tried to lighten the mood. "Are you hungry? There's some more soup in the kitchen. It should still be warm. After you eat I think you should go work on your aiming with your bow. Later, when Liz is feeling better we can make a couple targets and you can try double arrows. Then, after you master that, you can try flaming arrows for fun."

"Okay. That sounds fun." Jerriney left the room and went to the kitchen. Nerezzan came in.

"You want some soup?" Jerriney asked.

"Sure, why not," Nerezzan said after he hopped onto the table.

Jerriney got two bowls out and filled both with soup. She gave one to Nerezzan, placed her bowl next to his, then sat at the table and ate in silence.

✝ Chapter Six ✝

During the ambush, John and Tesa were taken captive. They were taken to an island north of Koder Docks and held in caves. They stared at the ceiling as water dripped from the slimy green and grey stalactites.

"How long have we been here?" Tesa asked John.

"I'm not sure. A day or more."

"We could have been back home with Jerriney by now." Tesa started crying. "I wonder what she looks like all grown up." John took her in his arms and held her.

"I'm sure we'll find a way out. We are in the king's secret service are we not?"

"Yes, but what about the goblins? We've faced goblins before, but not like this. Plus, we have no weapons."

"Maybe there is a different way out than the way we came in." John looked around for any signs of light.

A goblin walked in.

"The captain wishes to speak with you," the goblin said in a deep, rough voice.

John and Tesa got up and followed the goblin into a part of the cave that looked like some kind of hall.

They took a seat on rocks around a small fire. A man was sitting across from them.

"Thank you Gulgor. You may leave." The goblin left and then the man looked at John and Tesa. "Hello John, Tesa. I am Dashlegar Crainten. You might have a couple questions for me—"

"Where are we?" Tesa interrupted. "Why do you need us? Why did you stage an ambush?"

"You are on the island of Mordalla. I staged the ambush so I could get you two. You have something I want, nothing major, just five stones. Blue stones." The captain studied his fingernails.

John and Tesa glanced at each other.

"We don't have any blue stones," John calmly said as he stared into Dashlegar's eyes.

"Oh, you don't?" Dashlegar raised an eyebrow. "That's funny. I heard that they had been handed down through your family for generations."

John and Tesa were silent.

"Alright, I see you don't want to tell me where they are. Gulgor!"

The goblin rushed in. "Yes sir?"

"Search their belongings, then search them,"

Dashlegar ordered.

"Yes sir." The shiny objects tied to the goblin's belt clinked as he walked away.

"Where's Gozan?" Tesa asked.

"Oh he's safe, somewhere in the caves."

After a short while, Gulgor came back in. "No blue stones sir, but I did find this." Gulgar handed Dashlegar some papers.

"Ah! They are from the king. Jerriney? Is that your daughter? The package is sent. What's the package? The stones perhaps?"

"No, she is not our daughter. And they were just some souvenirs from Dolash," John lied.

"Gulgar! Take your men. Go to Ascillia and find someone for me. A girl called Jerriney. Find her and bring her to me in Shamar Neshmah. Make sure she has those stones with her."

"Yes mi lord. Uh, sir?" The goblin hesitated.

"What do you want?" Dashlegar snapped.

"What should I do if the girl is not there?"

"Report back to me and I'll give you further instructions."

"Yes sir!" Once the goblin turned his back sadness crossed his face.

"As for you, John and Tesa, you may stay with me

or roam around the caves. I'm leaving for Koder Docks tomorrow."

Dashlegar allowed John and Tesa, along with the other man he had already freed, to live because he did not see them as a threat, and even if they somehow happened to get to Jerriney before he did, that would just give him more of a competition. He looked at it like a game that he controlled.

John and Tesa just looked at the floor.

"Well, I'm going to go get me some food," Dashlegar said rather cheerfully as he stood up to leave.

After Dashlegar left, John asked Tesa, "What do you want to do? We can go find Gozan then find a way out, or find him and come back and go to Koder Docks with Dashlegar Crainten."

"Then maybe we could escape and find Jerriney," Tesa suggested as she unbraided her brown hair only to braid it again. Whenever Tesa felt determined she always braided her hair, whether it was already braided or not.

"Yes that sounds good. Let's go find Gozan." John smiled as he watched her fix her hair. It was one of the things that had caught his eye when they first met.

Before they left, they each took a log from the fire to light their way.

"Where should we start?" Tesa finished her braid and flung it behind her.

"Let's go back to where we were. I remember seeing a passage near the back."

So they went back to their holding area and found a passage leading to a huge hall with many pillars.

"This looks as if someone actually lived in here once." John put the light in front of him.

"Hey, look! There are torches on the wall. Maybe we should light them so we can find our way back," Tesa suggested.

"Good idea." John lit the torch nearest to him. "We'll light any torch or lamp we find as we go along."

"These look like Dwarven carvings. Maybe we'll find some interesting things along the way."

They moved on to the back of the hall which led to three rooms.

"Which should we enter?"

"The one that's open," John said, pointing out the obvious.

"Oh yes, of course. We might not be able to open the others and if Gozan went this way he probably wouldn't bother to close the doors."

"Exactly," John chuckled.

They entered the room to the left. There were many

shelves full of dust and very old books as well as several tables and two desks.

"It's too bad we can't take all these books with us. Loreen would love to add them to her library," John said as he looked at the old tomes.

"Yes, she would be mighty happy." Tesa smiled. "I miss home." She looked at John.

"Me too, Tesa, me too."

Gozan let out a sigh of relief as he stepped out of the cave and into the sunlight. He squinted at the bright rays of light coming from the sun. When he was captured along with John and Tesa they tried to fight back. John and Tesa were knocked out so he stopped fighting. They were taken to the island of Mordalla where they were put into a room inside a cave. Right after the goblins left, Gozan sneaked out into a back passage in hopes of finding a way out. Now that he did, he wanted to go back and get John and Tesa.

He went back into the cave and walked through the passage. He had to remember what way he had come because he had no way of marking his path. When he rushed out of the cave he was being held captive, he did not think to bring anything along except a torch. Then he remembered that there were sconces on the wall with unlit torches. He could have lit his way here. Gozan was never good a paying attention to his surroundings. That was the kind of thing he always left to John and Tesa.

Gozan turned around and began retracing his steps using his memory. He turned into a room that had been a great feasting hall. Gozan passed all the elaborately decorated stone chairs and tables. When he got out of the hall he stopped. Which way now? There were five hallways all leading to who knows where.

He sat down in a nearby chair. He needed to think hard. If he could not remember which door he came from he might not see John and Tesa ever again. He closed his eyes and rubbed his temples.

"Maybe if I sit here a while it'll all come back to me," he thought out loud.

"Should we pick a couple out for her?" Tesa browsed the shelves in the library they had wandered into.

"Well maybe one or two. That's all that will fit in the bag we have. And maybe a couple scrolls from over there." He pointed to a table with books, scrolls, blank parchments, and feather quills sitting on it.

They chose two books and managed to fit them in their bag. They started looking at the scrolls for something that might interest Loreen.

"Hey look! Here's a map! It looks like the shape of the island. Maybe it will help us." Tesa gave the scroll to John.

"Wow! It looks like the dwarves built tunnels under the whole island! Look, here's where we came in, the south cave. Here's the place we were held, the big hall, so this must be where we are now." As John talked he pointed to the places on the map.

They found a couple scrolls that they thought Loreen would like and put them in their bag. Then they took the map and walked to the end of the library where there were two doors.

"Okay, which door looks like it has been used recently?" John asked.

"Look! This door's handle is all dusty and the one over there isn't."

"So let's go through that one. It looks like it leads to a big room with several little sections for sleeping or something," John said as he looked at the map.

They went through the left door and entered a hallway. They lit the wall sconces as they went down the hallway to the room it led to.

"Okay. According to the map there are five doors in this room. Let's go straight and look for disturbed dust or any other clues to which way Gozan went."

John led the way forward. In the middle of the room there were three doors across from them. They looked at the doors, walls, and floors around them. The one on the left was shut and looked like it hadn't been used in ages. The one in the middle was open, but there were spider webs in the doorway so if anyone passed that way they would have wrecked it, but it was undisturbed so they went to the third door. It was cracked open a little. All the dust was settled and untouched.

"So he didn't go this way," John started. "There are two more doors—one on the far left and one on the right. Which one?"

"Let's go this way," Tesa said as she pointed to the left. "That one is closer to the west opening. He might have gone toward cool air or light."

"Good idea Tesa."

They walked over to the door and inspected it.

"Look, a handprint on the door." Tesa pointed out.

"Okay. Let's go."

Bojan heard someone coming down one of the halls. Could it be goblins? The captain? Some other monster? Or maybe John and Tesa!

"Let's hope it's John and Tesa," he thought to himself. He stood up, ready for whatever it may be just as the door started creaking open ...

† Chapter Seven †

It had been four days since the messenger was sent to Duvok to get the doctor. Jerriney and Ron had three and a half days left until they found out what was wrong with Liz. Jerriney decided to go see Loreen to get her mind off of Liz. Nerezzan padded along. When she arrived to Loreen's house she knocked on the door but no one answered. She went around the back and found her crouched over her garden.

"Hello Loreen."

"Oh, hello Jerriney! How are you? How's Liz?" Loreen stood up from her herb patch.

"I'm fine. Liz isn't any better, if not worse." Jerriney looked at what Loreen had been working on. It looked like she had got some new plants and were adding them to her garden.

"Oh I do wish I could help more, but since I don't recognize what is wrong with her I don't know what herbs would help. I don't want to give her something that might worsen her conditions." Loreen looked sympathetically at Jerriney.

"Hopefully the doctor will be here in a couple

days." Jerriney studied the plants fiercely. She was trying her hardest not to cry.

There was a short pause before Loreen broke the silence, "So. Why did you come here?"

"Well ..."

"Oh, the stones." Loreen interrupted. "I almost forgot about them! Come along now."

Loreen led Jerriney and Nerezzan through the back door. Jerriney had never been in the back half of the house and she was amazed at all the books and trinkets the old lady could stuff in her little shack. There were many things that she could not put a name to that had no resemblance to anything she had ever seen before. Some looked like they had no apparent reason to be made. She wondered if Loreen had some kind of magic.

"Is Loreen in contact with the Fae?" She wondered. The Fae were the spirits that inhabited all the elements of nature. *"Is she Fae herself? Nah, that's impossible. Or is it?"* Jerriney was not sure and was afraid to ask. If Loreen happened to be Fae she may not like the fact that someone knew. She may erase Jerriney's mind of all she knew that involved Loreen. Maybe, if she thought Jerriney a big enough threat, she would even kill her.

Fae folk were not very fond of humans. They

71

considered them to be disgusting, ugly, rude beings who just wanted to take the Fae's magic from them. Jerriney told herself that she would ask Nerezzan and see what he thought. He seemed to know everything.

Loreen led them into a study where there was a desk with several books, some papers, feather quills and an open book with Jerriney's blue stones on it. Loreen went over to the desk and sat down. She gently wiped the stones off the book and turned some pages.

"The stones are called Promotheans. They were used during the time that the Sur'donians thrived. Have you heard of them Jerriney?"

Jerriney shook her head. She had never heard of anything like that.

"Well Nerezzan knows quite a bit about them. I wouldn't be surprised if he was a Sur'donians companion once. The Sur'donians are better known around here as Stone Wielders. Does that sound familiar?"

"Yea, it was mentioned in one of the stories I heard as a young girl, but there weren't any specifics about them."

"Well they aren't called Stone Wielders for no reason. They took stones, like yours, and put them in bowls of dragons' tears where they soaked for many months. Dragons' tears are very powerful, for dragons only cry when the die. Those tears, only three or four per dragon, are full of all the magic left in that dragon. After the stones were soaked, they contained all the magic of that dragon. The Stone Wielders found ways to use this magic and at first they were prosperous and used them rarely and only for good. But one day, a group of young Stone Wielders wanted more power and to use the magic stones more often. They killed or drove off any in their way and murdered the old Stone Wielders who kept the rules and acted as leaders." Loreen flipped through the book again and scanned a passage to make sure she was telling the story correctly.

"Soon the king in Dolash heard of this news and saw it as a threat. He sent all his best men and their armies to destroy the Sur'donians and scatter the stones over the land of Dolash and Amensdale. They prevailed and the use of stones was demolished. But because the Sur'donians used the magic in the dragons' tears in a destructive way the dragons' trust with humans was destroyed." She closed the book and looked at Jerriney. "That is why you don't see dragons in the sky anymore. If someone were to take the stones to their leaders, the High Dragons, one would gain back the dragons' trust in humans if the one who brought the stones was pure

73

in heart. The only problem is no one has ever seen the leaders in a long time or even knows if they are still in Amensdale, though many have searched."

"Might they be dead?"

"No, the High Dragons are immune to death by age, which is why they are the leaders. Only magic or another dragon can kill them, but no dragon, even an evil one, would try to kill the High Dragons. If they did dragons would lose their wings and the ability to breathe fire."

"How did they get enough dragon tears for all the stones if only three or four fall per dragon?"

"The Sur'donians were also dragon breeders and when a dragon died they collected its tears, but they never purposely killed a dragon for if they did the dragons would not breed for them or let them collect their tears."

"I see. And were they just humans with magic stones?"

"Yes. Any human, elf, dwarf, whatever race, could use the stones."

Nerezzan suddenly jumped through a window and came up to Jerriney.

"Tell Loreen about the rock you found in the woods."

"How did you …"

"I'm a creature of magic. You don't need to tell me things. I read your mind. Hence the way I communicate."

Jerriney turned to Loreen.

"I was hunting deer the other day and found a blue stone similar to the ones my aunt and uncle sent me, only it had silver lines in it that seemed to be moving around."

"Let me see this stone. Have you got it with you?"

"Yes, I do." Jerriney searched her pockets. "Here it is."

Loreen took the stone.

"Hmm, just as I thought. Oh this *is* exciting!" Loreen walked closer to the window. "You see, this is not a stone you have picked up. Look!" She held the blue stone that was not a stone up to the light.

"It's transparent!" Jerriney exclaimed.

"Yes. This is a dragon's tear!"

"I thought dragons only cried when they died. There was not a dead dragon or bones around the place I found it."

"That is true, but I've read in legends that sometimes, very rarely, they cry for other reasons. But only a single tear at a time. And this one fell from the sky! If the dragon was on the ground the tear would just seep into the soil and the magic would be returned to the Earth. Miniscule elements in the air around us have a reaction with the magic and fuse with it making a sort of lining on the tear as it falls." Loreen looked at Jerriney and smiled at her.

"You are very lucky. Only two other people have found one. One was a king who was very fond of his dragon, and she of him. The king wished to have a tear from her encased in a gem to put on his sword so he would always have some of her with him, and so he could be buried with it. So she cried for him. The other was an elf. She was searching for herbs when she looked up and saw a group of dragons. She sensed in them a great sadness. Then suddenly she saw a glitter of light fall from the sky and lo and behold! A dragon tear! She took it and buried it near one of the dragons' graves, for elves have no use of dragon tears because elves are born with magic in their blood." She got up and went to her desk and swatted at a fly, hitting her thigh with a flat 'smack!'

"And now you are the third. That's why you, Jerriney, must go on the journey and return the dragon tear and the stones to the dragons' leader. Fate has chosen you for this deed. This dragon tear you found

76

must be a sign that it was no mistake those blue stones came to you." Loreen wiped the dead fly off her dirt covered skirt.

"But you said the person had to be pure in heart. How does one know?"

"Be true to yourself, follow your heart, and do not stray to the uses of Dark Magic. That should do you well. And remember, use the power of the stones if you should come upon temptation to help you choose the correct path." Loreen hugged her and said, "You are strong. I know you will be fine."

✝ Chapter Eight ✝

The steps were getting closer. Gozan crouched in a ready stance. The door slowly creaked open. *"Now!"* He raced forward only to find himself on the floor over John.

"Ow!" John said as he looked up at his squisher. "That hurt Gozan! Get off me!"

"Sorry, didn't know who it was."

John brushed some dust off his shirt.

"It's alright Gozan," Tesa said as she stepped forward. "At least we've found you."

"Yeah. I was coming back for you. I found a way out. Just beyond that hallway over there." He pointed back the way he came. "Come on! Let's go!"

"No! Gozan wait. We already have something planned. John and I discussed it back in the caves."

"Alright. What is it?"

John spoke now. "Dashlegar is leaving for Koder Docks tomorrow. We will ride with them to the mainland and from there we'll find a way to escape and go find Jerriney to warn her."

"Are you sure that's safe?"

"No, but we have no other way to get across the water to Kodar Docks."

"Oh. That's right. Well then, shall we go?"

After Jerriney and Loreen were done talking, Jerriney decided she would go and search for the dragons that Loreen mentioned once the doctor came and treated Liz. Loreen told her never to leave the stones anywhere unattended even if she was coming back soon, and to always carry them on her when she left the house. She was to take Nerezzan with her to help guide and answer questions. She also needed to take her weapons.

Jerriney was a little afraid but she was determined to find a dragon.

"I have given Nerezzan some information as to what you are to do when you find a dragon. He will tell you when he thinks the time is right," Loreen told her and set her on her way.

"Get those crates on board!" Dashlegar yelled at his goblin workers from the mouth of the cave. "I want to leave before the day is out. We need to get to the girl before someone else does!"

"Excuse me, mi lord, but who else would be looking for the girl?" Gulgor asked Dashlegar.

"Well how would I know Gulgor? Unless they're utterly stupid they would keep their mission a secret. If I were to find out of anyone I would kill them instantly. There may be someone else who knows that our employer wants the stones and is trying to get them before I do so they can get a reward. It's also best to get there as soon as possible in case she has someone who can tell her of our coming which would make her flee." Dashlegar flicked at a large bug that had just fell onto his shoulder from the ceiling of the cave.

"Oh. There's a reward for these stones?"

"Yes, but I did not take it."

"In all due respect mi lord, how come!"

"Gulgor, you know I take jobs from everywhere. Although I do love gold and have a rich amount of it, I do not take these jobs for the material things. I take them for the pleasure and adventure of being immortal."

"Gulgor would take the gold," the goblin muttered

80

under his breath, thinking his master would not hear him.

"Of course you would Gulgor. Goblins would trade their own mother in for a shiny object. If I coated my poo in gold paint you would take it. Now go make sure everyone is working as fast as they can." Gulgor slunk off, silently cursing his master.

𝕵oljn, Tesa, and Gozan had made their way through the tunnels and were watching Dashlegar yell orders at goblins that were loading crates on to two large ships.

"I wonder what's in all those crates," Gozan said in a hushed voice.

"Probably their loot and plunder they have accumulated and hidden here. The gifts from King Haldor to our king are probably somewhere in their possession," Tesa stated.

"Do you think we can grab them before we escape?" Gozan asked, figuring they'd be even more praised on their return when the king finds out that they are alive *and* they managed to retrieve the goods.

"We should focus on escaping first. It's more important for us to return to the king alive and tell him what Dashlegar is up to then it is for him to get the gifts back." Tesa answered him.

"It looks like they're about done loading the ships," John said. "We should get aboard before Dashlegar changes his mind and decides to leave us here."

So John, Tesa, and Gozan boarded the ship and tried to figure out what to do once they arrived at Koder Docks.

† Chapter Nine †

"**So** how do I use the stones' powers?" Jerriney asked Loreen. She had come with Nerezzan to see Loreen the day after she had told her what the stones were to get her mind off Liz again.

"No one but the wielder knows. Every person has their own style. There are accounts of people holding them to channel the power where some preferred to have them in a bag at their side or there was even one I read about where he kept them hidden at home. Whenever he wanted to use their power he closed his eyes and focused on that spot. Of course I can't imagine that would be very useful if you are in a hurry. You will most likely have to practice channeling the power before you get the hang of it. Start with something small like trying to lift a small pebble or making water ripple. The power you will have once you master it will be beyond measure. You will be able to conjure fire out of seemingly nothing and hurl it at your enemies. I read, out of the same book, that one stone wielder even found a way to make himself blend in with his environment and even fly! Nerezzan may be able to help you. I am pretty sure he already has some knowledge on these Promotheans, whether or not he has told you. I will also speak with him and tell him what I have gathered from my brother's books." Loreen started to go through the disarray of papers on her desk. Jerriney just stood there for a moment speechless.

"Are you alright dear?" Loreen asked, pausing in her attempt to organize the shambolic desk.

"Yes, I'm fine. It's just a lot to take in all at once," Jerriney slowly said.

"I agree, it is, but I'm telling you everything now because we don't have much time. You must leave before the sun falls tomorrow. I have been meditating and the stars have told me that someone is coming, searching for you—for these stones. You must leave before they get here. I did not wish to tell you this because I did not want to frighten you, but I think it is necessary now so that you move as quickly as possible and put as much ground as you can between you and these men."

"A-alright. What must I take? Where will I go?" Jerriney couldn't believe that just the other day she was wishing she could go on some big adventure. Now she was frightened. Her eyes suddenly widened.

"What about Liz? She's sick. I can't leave her

now!"

Loreen put a comforting hand on Jerriney's shoulder. "Do not worry about Elizibeth, dear." She then returned to rummaging about her desk.

"You won't need to take many things. Bring your sword, your bow and arrows, and your stones of course. Take a small bag with a blanket and some necessary tools like skinning knives and small cups and some food that will last a while. Nerezzan will no doubt come with you. Don't try to make him stay—it is not your choice. You know how he is. And make sure you take all the coins you can. Since you can't carry much I'm sure you'll want to buy provisions at any chance you can. As far as where you should go, I do not know, but I think you should start at the Abbey near Duvok and look for a monk called Demeter. He was once chosen by the gods to write a prophecy. See what he has to say."

They were both silent for a while, Jerriney not knowing what to say and Loreen giving her a chance to let all this settle. Once Jerriney didn't look so pale, Loreen nudged her out the door.

"Go on, dear. You have a destiny to fulfill!"

"Thank you, Loreen, I will search for the High Dragons," Jerriney said, suddenly filled with great confidence and courage. "Come on Nerezzan."

"I'll send Nerezzan home later. I have a few things I wish to discuss with him before you leave for Duvok."

Jerriney left for home wondering how she was going to restore the trust of humans to the dragons alone and worrying deeply about Liz. Something didn't feel right.

𝕵erriney returned home quickly. She didn't know why, but for some reason she felt she needed to get there as fast as she could. There was an eerie silence about the house when she reached the porch. She hesitantly opened the door and cautiously walked in. There was no one in the kitchen or around the fireplace. There wasn't even a fire going, which was unusual for this time of day.

"That's odd," she thought. "Ron always has the fire going by now." The empty fireplace left the house cold. As she rubbed her goose bumps away, she felt like she was in one of Loreen's scary stories about shadowy demons on the walls that entered human bodies and made their life a living hell.

"Hello?" She quietly called out. "Was that whimpering I just heard?"

"Jerriney!" Ron practically screamed as he came running out of his and Liz's room. He looked horrible. He was still in his wood chopping clothes. Clearly he had been in a hurry when he had finished chopping this weeks' firewood. There was dirt smeared over his face still and his hair was a mess. You never saw him unkempt in the house. He was always clean and tidy unless he was working. As she strained against the dark to get a better look at his face she noticed there were streaks on his dirt-covered face.

"He's been crying." She realized. "What's wrong? Is Liz okay?" She found it hard to speak. It felt like her stomach was caught in her throat.

"She …she's …" Ron couldn't even finish his sentence before he collapsed to his knees. Jerriney rushed forward and joined him on floor, holding him. "She's gone." Jerriney caught him say between sobs.

She got up and went to Ron and Liz's room. Liz was lying there. Serene. Jerriney touched her face. There was still a little color left in her cheek, but it felt drained of heat. She flinched at the unfamiliar coldness. The past couple days Liz had been burning up with a fever. It was strange how quickly all that heat had disappeared.

Jerriney couldn't cry at first. The tears were stuck

in her throat. She didn't know for sure if this was real or if she was in a dream. It all seemed so alien. The house: all dark and void of life. Liz. She looked so peaceful, a smile played on her blue-tinged lips. Ron, in the hallway, weeping. Ron was always the chipper one. He was always cheering everybody up. You would think there wasn't a sad bone in his body. Yet here he was, broken and grief struck. Jerriney found her legs wouldn't hold her any longer. She fell into the chair at side of the bed. The tears came freely now.

She woke not long after she fell asleep and the moon was still high in the sky. She was still in the chair beside Ron and Liz's bed except now there was a sheet over her. There was also a sheet over the bed with the form of a human under it.

"Liz," Jerriney murmured as she remembered the night's events. She stood up and went into the living room. The fire was going now and two figures were sitting in the chairs around it talking in hushed voices. One voice was filled with sorrow. She walked closer. The other figure turned around.

"Jerriney dear come here." Loreen beckoned her. Jerriney ran into her outstretched arms and curled up in Loreen's lap like she used to do when she was a child.

"When you left, Nerezzan told me about Elizibeth.

I'm sorry I couldn't do anything about it." Loreen stroked Jerriney's hair as a mother would to console a weeping child.

"You don't need to be s-sorry," Jerriney said between sobs. "No one knew what it was. You couldn't have done anything without risking making her worse." Nerezzan jumped up on Jerriney and joined the pile. Cats always know when you need a good cuddling.

"It is still very important that you leave before midday. It is just reaching the peak of the night so you don't have much time. I have spoken with Ron and he is to go with you. It has been decided between Ron and I that it would be best to burn Elizibeth and put her ashes in a jar for you to hold a memorial upon your return. I would preserve her as she is now, but I fear this journey will take you far too long for her to stay in her current form without a proper burial, so burning seems the only choice. I know this is hard to do right now Jerriney, but we must move. You have a very important job to do, and only you can do it."

Jerriney sniffled. "Alright." She still couldn't believe that Liz was actually gone and really did not wish to leave so soon. But then she remembered what Loreen had said before she returned home. There were men after her. Who knew what they would do to her and Ron to get what they wanted? Jerriney got up and went to pack for the road ahead.

𝔚hen she had finished packing it was still dark out. Ron said she should try and get some sleep. Once the sun had risen above the horizon Ron woke her up.

"Let's go, Jerri. Loreen sounded pretty frightened of the men that are coming." They went outside. Ron already had the horses ready with their things packed on.

"Where's Nerezzan?" Jerriney asked.

"Mrwar," Nerezzan replied, choosing to respond in his "I'm here!" meow rather than speak.

"How will he travel with us?" Jerriney asked Ron.

"While you were sleeping I made something I'm hoping will work." He showed her what looked like a sort of basket, but with shortened walls.

"He sits in here and you place it in front of the horn on your saddle. These straps here attach to the saddle and these ones go around the horse's neck so it stays in place," Ron said as he showed her how to put it on.

"I also made this little lid to put over him when it's raining or if he just wants to be covered."

"I think that will work quite nicely. Thanks, Ron."

Jerriney looked back at the house, wondering if she would ever see it again.

"We will be back soon enough," Ron said, as if he had read her mind.

"I don't think we need anything else so we will go right through Ascillia and on to Kale," Ron told Jerriney as she got on her horse. "If we hurry we can make it before sunset. We'll stop for a short rest and then stay in the inn once we get to Kale. Then we'll continue on to Duvok."

Ron and Jerriney were both quiet for a while, as if pondering something. Jerriney looked back at the house, then at Ron. He was making sure the straps on the horses were all on correctly and that the horses were comfortable in their saddles. Last night he seemed so devastated and broken. Now he seemed almost normal. After what happened yesterday, with Liz dying, he didn't seem deterred by it at all. This worried Jerriney.

"Ron?" she asked quietly.

"Yes, what is it dear?" Ron looked up from the horse.

"Are you okay? I mean with Liz and all. You were really upset last night. I've never seen you like that before and now, well, it's almost like nothing happened." She looked at the mane of her horse and

91

watched the wind tussle it lightly.

"I am still very upset. Never in my entire life did I meet someone as, as perfect as Elizibeth. Never have I loved someone as much as I loved—still love—her. She did so much for me, sacrificed so much for me. She was actually born into a fairly rich family. When she met me and we started talking about marriage, I didn't think she would do it because I was just a poor woodworker. Her family was even opposed to our union. They said she would get no inheritance if she tainted the family blood with a commoner like me. She still married me, without any hesitance. She could have had everything she ever wanted, everything I couldn't afford to give her. She had such a kind heart. I'm sure she still does wherever she may be. I did not lose her, she merely moved into my heart. I will always have her with me, no matter where I go. So I do not need to be sad anymore. We need to focus on the path that is ahead of us," Ron reassured her.

"I see. That makes me happier to know that she hasn't really left us. I never knew about her family. Thank you for telling me." Jerriney smiled at Ron.

"Alright. Let's go," Ron said as he set Nerezzan in his basket in front of Jerriney.

† Chapter Ten †

"**I** don't 'ave any ridin' horses," said a short, gruff, old man, "but you can 'ave Betsy and Clyde here." He patted the back of an older brown mare that was standing next to her grey companion. "I used 'em with me plow before I sold me farm so I'm not sure how fast they'll go, but they'll get'cha wherever you're goin' well enough. For a few gold pieces you can keep 'em."

John, Tesa, and Gozan had escaped easily enough. Dashlegar didn't seem to care much what happened to them, and didn't say a word to them or even have any of his men subdue them when they left. Now they were trying to get some horses so they could beat Dashlegar and his men to Ascillia before they got a hold of Jerriney.

"We'll take them," Tesa told the man. John got out his coin purse, they had managed to get their things back before they left the ship, and gave the old man more than enough for the two horses.

"We'd like those saddles over there as well. Don't

think you'll be needing them now without the horses," John said as gestured towards the two saddles that were hung on the wall. The man agreed and they got the horses saddled and went on their way.

"Wait," Gozan said. "There are three of us and two horses."

"Ah, that might be a problem," Ron replied. "Well, Tesa is light enough, maybe she and I can ride Clyde here and you can take Betsy."

"All the way to Ascillia? Usually it would take three days. These horses are pretty old and aren't used to being ridden, so it might take an extra day. I don't think either of them can take two riders."

"Gozan makes a good point," Tesa stated.

"Here's what I propose," Gozan started. "Since you haven't seen Jerriney in years and you need to get to her, you two go on to Ascillia without me. I will find myself a horse and ride to Morga. I'm sure Dashlegar has told the king that we were killed. He would be upset with us if we did not get word to him as soon as we can that we are alive and Dashelgar is up to something."

"You always have things fully thought through Gozan." John clasped his friend's shoulder. "I'm glad to have served with you and hope to see you in the future."

"As am I." Tesa gave Gozan a hug. "Although I do not wish to go on another mission anytime soon. We have many things to catch up with Jerriney." She grabbed John's hand and smiled lovingly at him.

"Alright then. To Morga I go!" Gozan smiled at them and waved them goodbye as he strode into the busy streets of Koder.

After a day of riding, Jerriney and Ron arrived in Kale.

"I think it would be wise to stop at a local blacksmith and get our blades sharpened. From what Loreen said, we might be needing them," Ron told Jerriney.

"Alright. Let's find an inn first. Nerezzan said he doesn't want to go with us to the blacksmith. He doesn't care for the smell." So they dropped Nerezzan off at the inn before continuing on to the blacksmith.

"Can I help you with something sir?" Said a young man as he put down a hammer and picked up a cloth to wipe the sweat from his face. The cloth already had smudges on it from being used throughout the day so it only smeared the dirt on his face.

Jerriney assessed him as Ron told him what all he

needed done. She figured he had to be about two years older than her. His hair was dirty blonde, wavy, and unkempt and he had beautiful blue eyes. He was tall and muscular, obviously from working at the blacksmith.

After Ron had told him what they needed and handed him their swords he looked at Jerriney. She realized she had been staring wide-eyed at him and quickly looked down. Blushing, she took a peek back up and saw him smiling as he turned around.

"What a gorgeous smile," she thought.

Since Jerriney and Ron picked up supplies on their way to the blacksmith, they didn't really have anything else to do in Kale, so they stayed at the blacksmiths and waited while he sharpened their swords and took the dents out.

"What brings you two to Kale?" The young man was obviously a very friendly person. "My name is Drust by the way."

"We are on our way to the Abbey by Duvok to get some information," Ron answered him.

"Just the two of you?" Jerriney was glad he didn't press about what kind of information. It was hard enough trying to understand their situation herself without having to explain to someone else that they were basically trying to save all of Amensdale.

"Um, yes." Ron seemed confused by Drust's concern that they were going to Duvok. "Is there something wrong with that?"

"Well, no. That is, if you can put these swords to use. Duvok is going through some hard times right now and is filled with thugs and street rats. If you're not careful you can get the clothes stolen right off your back or even be killed. But if you've been there recently and know the safer places then you'll be fine."

"I haven't been to Duvok since I was a kid," Ron said as he scratched the back of his head. Jerriney could tell this worried him quite a bit.

"Do you know of anyone who could be a guide for us?" Jerriney asked Drust.

"There aren't many people who go there now-a-days because of all the crime. But I know my way around the place. I go there often to get supplies for the shop. Actually we're in need of some re-stocking. If you want I can take you there and show you a good inn and a safe route to the Abbey."

"You'd be willing to do that for a couple of strangers?" Ron asked him.

"We'll you seem like honest people and I could use the company." He looked at Jerriney when he said the last part. She couldn't help not to blush.

"What about the man who owns this blacksmith? Don't you get company from him?"

"Gordon, he's the old man who owns this place, isn't really around much and he's not all too friendly and there aren't any other workers. If it weren't for me he'd probably drive off his customers with his grumpy mood." He had finished with Ron's blade and switched to Jerriney's.

Ron wasn't so sure about letting a complete stranger show them around an unfamiliar place. What if this kid had some devious plan to gain their trust and, just when they least expect it, rob them of all they had?

"What are you thinking Ron? This young man not only sharpened our swords, but also took the dents out and shined the blade! I didn't ask him to do that! He seems like a good kid. Plus, if I need to leave Jerriney, he could protect her. Maybe he'd help us with our journey ..."

"Alright, Drust. We would be glad to have someone show us the less corrupt areas of Duvok." Ron finally answered him after a couple awkward moments of silence.

"Then it's set. Let me just tell Gordon and run home and grab some things. Can I meet you at the inn in the morning?" Drust seemed pretty excited to be joining them.

"Sounds good," Ron told him as he took the blades from Drust. Jerriney and Ron then returned to the inn.

† Chapter Eleven †

"**What's** the problem now, Gulgor!" Dashlegar yelled at the goblin.

"It seems, mi lord, that your mount has a lame back leg, mi lord." Gulgor was tired of being yelled at all day and was trying to stay on the captain's good side.

"Well don't just sit there! Get me a new mount!" They had left Koder two days ago and he had already gone through three horses. He pushed the animals hard and didn't let them rest long because he wanted to get to Ascillia and the stones as quickly as possible. He had sent out some men ahead of him to secure the girl and whoever may be protecting her so he could get the stones and leave without a struggle.

"They better have found the girl and those stones," he thought to himself angrily.

"There aren't any farms around here, mi lord," Gulgor said while he writhed his hands together. The last time Dashlegar had become angry he beheaded one of the sailors who had come with them. The goblin hoped he would not choose to behead another. Gulgor always had to clean up after him and he hated the smell.

"I'll take his then." Dashlegar pointed at one of his men. "You there! Give me your horse!" The man hesitantly got off his horse and handed it to Gulgor. Dashlegar dismounted his horse.

"We'll stay here for the night and continue for Gurda Valley in the morning."

𝕵erriney, Ron, and Drust had left that morning for Duvok and were staying on the edge of the forest for the night. They had already eaten and were sitting around the fire.

Drust was telling them about his family. His parents had died when he was nine. Their house caught on fire and they were unable to escape. Drust was out playing in the woods at the time. When he came home all that was left was rubble. There was a couple who lived close by that had seen the smoke and came as fast as they could but they were too late. Drust stayed with them until the man came home one day from his work in town and told him he met someone who had a job offer for Drust. Ever since he was ten he had worked in the blacksmith shop at Kale.

"Don't you ever get tired of doing the same thing

over and over every year?" Jerriney asked him.

"It's not that bad." He shrugged. "It keeps my mind from thinking about my parents or other things that are going wrong in my life. It doesn't just make me physically strong, it makes me mentally strong too."

"Did they ever find out what started the fire?" Ron questioned Drust.

"Nah. I don't think anyone really tried figuring out what happened. There was a funeral and then that was it. Everyone seemed to forget there was ever a house and family there."

"That's so sad. I—" Jerriney said. She was going to say more but Ron cut her off.

"Shh!" Ron held a finger to his lips. "Did you guys hear that?"

"What is it?" Drust asked.

"Steel upon steel, and shouting. Someone's fighting over that way." He gestured east.

"Should we check it out?" Jerriney was a little excited at the thought of using her sword for real instead of sparring, but she was also fearful.

"We'll take a peek. If our help is needed we will aid them. Follow me. Stay low and be quiet," Ron ordered.

They soundlessly crept closer to where all the

ruckus was coming from. Once the noise was almost right in front of them Ron gestured them to stop and lay low. He peeked over the bushes. There were four men. Three of them were obviously bandits. The fourth, the one they must have ambushed, was young, not much older than Jerriney. By the way he was dressed he had to be quite wealthy. He had black hair and his skin was darker than most around this part of the world. The young man was good with a sword as well. He soon overcame one of the bandits.

Ron whispered to the two to return to the camp. "I'll see if he needs any help and then return."

Jerriney and Drust returned to the camp. Ron then rushed out of the bushes at the closest bandit. The remaining two where easily subdued.

"Thank you sir, but I'm sure I could have handled it myself," the young man said to Ron.

"I could tell by the way you handled your blade that you were not in need of my assistance, but I noticed you were alone. Traveling by yourself can be dangerous, especially in the forest where dangers could be hiding behind every bush and tree."

"Ah, well thank you for your concern. I'm traveling to Duvok. I have become bored of living on my uncle's estate. I want to experience real life."

103

"What's your name boy?"

"I am called Muirnen."

"Well, Muirnen, Duvok is not what it once was. I do not think it wise to start a new life there. It has become crime-ridden. I suggest you do not go in alone." Ron sheathed his sword and surveyed Muirnen's encampment.

"I had not heard that Duvok had succumbed to crime. I heard stories when I was young of it being a beautiful and prosperous town."

"Ah yes, and it used to be. I have not seen it myself in many years but my daughter and I are traveling to Duvok as well and we passed through Kale and met a young blacksmith who journeys there often who told us of Duvok's unfortunate circumstances. He is with us now. He is going to show us the safest parts of town. Perhaps you would like to join us? You can see the city yourself and decide if you still wish to stay there."

"That is very gracious of you. I will accept your offer, that is, if it is okay with your companions."

"They will be fine with it." Ron started to put out the fire Muirnen had going.

"Come join us at our camp." Muirnen packed up his things and followed Ron back to Jerriney and Drust.

"There's no one here, Sire," a middle-aged, bald man told Dashlegar. Three of his men on some of the fastest horses in the country had ridden ahead to secure the girl and the stones before he arrived in Ascillia. They were now at a quaint little house on the edge of the Tokenda Forest.

"Are you sure this is where the girl lives?" Dashlegar walked into the seemingly deserted house. "It looks as if the inhabitants of this house have not been here for quite some while."

"Yes, mi lord, this is the place. She was sent here after her aunt and uncle left on that mission," Gulgor told Dashlegar. "Someone must have told them we were coming and left before your men got here."

"That's impossible. Absolutely no one could have known of our coming here." Dashlegar was looking out the kitchen window. "Who could have told them?!" He slammed his fist on the sink counter in frustrated rage. "This was supposed to be an easy capture. It was so simple! We were supposed to just walk in here, kill the family, and take the stones. You buffoons had to go and mess it up! Why must I do everything myself if it is to be done right?"

Gulgor looked at the men who had come here ahead of the rest. He felt a little sorry for them. He

105

knew there was no way they could have prevented the girl from leaving, and so did Dashlegar; nevertheless, he would probably have them killed for this.

"Alright." Dashlegar turned around to face his men. "Look through the house. See if there's anything of value. Then burn it down." He started walking out of the house then he stopped in front of the three men who had ridden ahead. "As for you three, I'll deal with you later. Right now I need you to go to Kale and pick up my new suit from the tailor. Then wait for me in Durma." He then left the house.

"Gulgor!"

"Yes, mi lord?" The goblin rushed after Dashlegar.

"We'll watch the house burn then we'll go to Kale. See if anyone at the bar has seen this girl. You know her name and description correct?" Dashlegar picked at his teeth.

"Yes sir, along with the names and descriptions of the couple she was living with."

"Good. You can keep your worthless life then."

Drust had successfully navigated Jerriney, Ron, and Muirnen through the grimy streets of Duvok to a fairly decent inn. They were jumped three times in the process, but they easily overpowered the robbers without killing them.

One of the ambushes was a bit harder for them to overcome and they should have lost, but, as Drust put it, luck was on their side. *"I don't quite think it was luck,"* Muirnen had commented to himself.

There were half a dozen cutpurses that obviously were seasoned in the trade. Jerriney was attacked by a behemoth and did not look to be faring well, then all of a sudden Muirnen felt a change in the air. He looked at Jerriney.

She kicked the man's leg while he was recovering from a strike. Muirnen saw a faint blue outline on Jerriney's shin and the thief went flying when he should have just fell to the ground. *"She's tapping into her power unconsciously. Normally demi-gods can't use their power without knowing that they are doing so. I imagine she would be very powerful if someone taught her how to control her magic. Probably even invincible."* Muirnen had made a mental note not to make her angry, in case she accidentally leaked magic into her rage. Once they were finished with that group, the rest of the way to the inn was clear.

"Alright, tomorrow Jerriney and I will go to the Abbey and see if we can find the, uh, information we need," Ron told Drust and Muirnen. "You two can go do whatever you need to do here in town. Then I'm guessing we'll go our separate ways."

"Now that I have seen the town, I do not think I want to live here anymore," Muirnen said. "Would you mind if I tag along with you when you leave this place until I find somewhere that's more livable?" he asked Ron.

"We'll discuss that when we get back from the Abbey. I would love to help you find a new home but it depends on what Jerri and I find out from the monks."

"I don't mean to pry, but what type of information are you looking for anyway?" Drust asked.

"Let's just say it's serious enough that I do not know if we should share it with anyone," Ron answered him. He hoped that neither Drust nor Muirnen would further ask about what they were up to.

"Once we find out more information, then we'll decide if we can tell you or not. You deserve that at least for helping us," Jerriney told Drust.

"Alright. Sounds good to me." Drust laid down on one of the cots. They all settled down for the night.

$\mathfrak{The}$ next morning Jerriney and Ron headed off for the Abbey. Drust had told them about the safest route before they left. Nerezzan said he wished to stay at the inn.

"I don't like to be around those dusty libraries and chanting monks," he told Jerriney. So they left him in the room, basking in the sun on the windowsill.

Ron and Jerriney would be gone for most of the day. Before they left, Jerriney told Drust and Muirnen to tell Nerezzan where they were going if they left. They asked her why they needed to tell a housecat what they were going to do.

"Because he's some kind of magical cat and he likes to know what people are up to. Right Zan?" She turned around too look at the large, black cat. He meowed in acknowledgement. She left them in complete confusion before they could ask any more questions.

"Alright well I'm going for a walk. Here that cat?" Muirnen raised his voice slightly louder as if it would help him understand.

"I swear that cat just rolled his eyes," Drust said to himself. "Wait, Muirnen!" He yelled after him but he was already out of the inn. "Why is he going for a walk

alone in a town he knows is dangerous?" he said out loud.

"Me-rawr!" The cat said, seeming to answer Drust. *"Maybe he has other intentions."* Drust couldn't tell if he thought that himself or if it somehow came from somewhere else. He looked at the cat.

"Magical eh?" Drust walked over to Nerezzan and stroked his long, soft, shiny fur. Nerezzan closed his eyes and purred.

"I remember hearing stories from my parents about magic in the world. Elves, dragons, stuff like that. There was this one story, it was my favorite, and it had a mighty dragon and a human who, with the help of the dragon, saved several other dragons from eternal imprisonment. And the best part was when—" He stopped suddenly. "Why am I speaking to a cat? Oh Drust, you must be going crazy." Drust wasn't so sure he was wrong in doing so though. It felt strangely right talking to Nerezzan. The cat seemed like he was listening. He had even stopped purring when Drust started talking about his memory and looked at him with his bright, blue eyes. Blue. "That's strange. All the black cats I've seen have orange eyes." The cat resumed his purring.

"Maybe you really are magic." Drust stood there

petting Nerezzan for a while thinking about all the things that he used to believe about as a child. "Maybe those stories have more truth to them than we think."

"Well I'm going to go get some things that the blacksmith in Kale needs, alright Nerezzan? Don't tell anyone, but I think I'll go with Jerri and Ron too. I actually told Gordon before we left Kale that I wouldn't be returning, but I'll send him the stuff he needs. Well, I'll be going if they allow me to." Nerezzan seemed to purr louder at this, as if in approval. Drust grabbed his pack and left the inn.

"𝕳ow are things going with the girl," said a rich, seductive voice that seemed to come from everywhere and nowhere all at once. Muirnen had ducked into the darkest ally he could find that was away from daily life.

"Not well, Mother. It's impossible to get close to her with Ron around. He protects her like she's his real daughter. Even if I had good intentions it would be difficult," Muirnen said to the empyreal voice.

"I'll take care of him. Make sure you stay with them. If they don't let you continue traveling with them you must follow them in secret. What are they doing now?"

"They went to the Abbey. Do you know what they are up to?" he asked.

"That is not your concern. Focus on the task ahead." The voice resounded through his very core. He noticed anger in her voice this time. "Go follow them. Report back to me before they leave Duvok."

"Yes, Mother." Muirnen turned around and left the alley.

𝕵errine𝔂 and Ron had arrived at the Abbey and were warmly welcomed in. They asked if a monk called Demeter was around. The monk that greeted them at the door said he was not sure if he was still at the Abbey. He told them that Demeter was planning on visiting his sister and would be away for a while but he did not know when exactly he was leaving. He sent them off to the library since that was where Demeter spent a good deal of his time.

The library was the most magnificent thing Jerriney had ever seen. She had never really gotten into reading as she was more interested in nature, but this room held so much knowledge and looked so glorious, in that old kind of way, that she couldn't help losing her breath.

"I've never seen so many books!" Jerriney exclaimed.

"We are quite proud of our collection here," said a monk that neither Ron nor Jerriney had noticed when they first walked in.

"Hello, I am Ron and this is Jerriney," Ron said to the monk.

"I am Brother Anthony. Welcome to our holy library. What can I help you with?"

"We were told we could find a monk named Demeter here," Ron explained. "Is he around?"

"Ah yes, he comes here quite often. He is not here right now though. He left moments ago. I am afraid he will not be back for a while. When he left he was mumbling something about his sister and that he must get to her quickly."

"Oh. Well that is most unfortunate. We were hoping to speak to him about some prophecy he wrote." Ron looked around at the many desks and scrolls lying around. Maybe they could still get some information.

"Ah, I see. Well, I can show you all his work he has done here. Maybe there you can find what you are looking for." Brother Anthony led them to desk that was larger than the others. There were papers on the desk with writings on some and grand pictures on

113

others. Clearly someone had been in the process of illustrating something before they left.

"This is Brother Demeter's work station. He was busy scrawling something down before he left." He moved around the desk and stood in front of it, motioning to the many scrolls on the shelves on the wall.

"These are his writings. I'm afraid it's not very organized. He tends to write things and then throw them up there once he has perfected them. We are meaning to put them into books, but as I'm sure you noticed, Duvok is not doing well and in turn the Abbey is not doing so well either. Therefore, we do not have the coin to afford the price of the printing press. I have taken my time to begin labeling the shelves in the year and month he produced them." He pointed at the edges of the shelves. Etched in several places among the shelves were two sets of numbers. "Don't worry about breaking the seals. Just place them on my desk when you leave and I will reseal them."

"Thank you, Brother Anthony, I'm sure this will help us," Ron said to the man. The monk then left them to wade through the many scrolls.

Jerriney was looking at the numerous piles of scrolls running her finger along the shelf when something made her stop. She looked at the stack in front of her. There were quite a lot under this month and year. She noticed there was a series of scrolls that were tied with the same deep green ribbon and gold detailed seal that looked like it had a dragon twining in a circle on it. Jerriney felt a strange pull towards them. She picked one up.

"Hey, Ron. Let's try this one." She handed it to him. Ron undid the seal and ribbon. He started skimming the words, reading to himself until he came upon something he thought was important.

"It tells about a man with a black heart, and a girl, and—" Ron suddenly stopped reading.

"What is it?"

"It mentions blue stones. Jerriney, I think this is talking about you."

✝ Chapter Twelve ✝

Dashlegar walked into a musty bar. Kale was a small village and the only place for travelers to stay was in the rooms above the bar. If Jerriney came through this way she would have stayed here.

"What can I get you today, sir?" the bartender asked him.

"I need to ask a couple of questions. Do you work here regularly?"

"Every day, every night."

"Has a girl with silver hair and emerald eyes come through here?" Dashlegar asked the man.

"Now, I don't think I should be releasing that kind of information, sir. I don't mean no harm, but I don't know you and I don't know what kind of man you are. You may be fixin' to kill the poor girl for all I know," the man said as he dried a mug.

"No, no, no, you've got me all wrong. See, I am her favorite uncle. I was planning a surprise visit, but her foster parents must have taken her on a little trip as they were not at their house," Dashlegar said

116

nonchalantly. If you didn't know him you would have thought he was speaking the truth.

"Oh, I'm sorry sir. Just to make sure, what is her name?"

"Jerriney," Dashlegar said, not hesitating to make sure it sounded like he had known the name for a lifetime rather than just learning of it a few days ago.

"Alright," the man replied. He smiled and seemed to loosen up. "A young woman with that description did come by here several days ago. She was with an older man who I assumed was her father, foster father, as you mentioned. They stayed the night and left early in the morning."

"How many days ago?"

"I'd say about two." He placed the mug under the counter.

"Thank you. Your information has been most helpful." Dashlegar smiled menacingly as he left the bar. Gulgor was waiting outside for him.

"What did he say? Where do we go now?"

"We head for Duvok. I reckon she wants to know more about the stones. The Abbey is the first place she'd look," Dashlegar said, ignoring the goblin's eagerness. They got on their mounts and left Kale.

"So, according to this prophecy, I am to speak to dragons, master the power of the stones, defeat this evil man, and ultimately save not only Amensdale, but the whole world!" Jerriney said to Drust, Muirnen, and Nerezzan. Ron and she had returned from the Abbey just before nightfall and explained to them what was going on. They figured they might be in need of some help with this little adventure if they were to succeed for it sounded like they might run in to trouble up ahead.

"Wow, it sounds like you were destined to be something you never imagined," Drust commented.

"No kidding. I would never have guessed that I would be doing this, or that I was so important to the future of this land." Jerriney was a little nervous with the fact that if she did not do this right than all of Amensdale and beyond would become corrupt.

"It sounds to me like you could use some help. I imagine there will be many men out to kill you," Muirnen said. He seemed unsurprised by this sudden news that Jerriney was to be savior or destroyer of this world.

"Yes, that is true Muirnen. We ask if you two strong, young men would join us on our journey. We

118

sure could use your swords," Ron said to them.

"I was hoping you'd ask that," Drust replied and smiled. Muirnen merely nodded.

"Alright then. We leave at sunrise." Then they all slept for what may be the last warm, calm night for days to come.

Once everyone was asleep, Muirnen got up and left the inn. He didn't go far like he had previously that day for he knew he would not be interrupted at this time of night. Instead he went to the stable that was near the inn.

"Mother, I have more news on the girl," he said to the dark.

"What is it, my son?" Her voice enveloped him.

"I followed them to the Abbey like you said. I went in a different way to be sure they did not see me and I saw a monk leaving."

"What does this have to do with the girl? I do not have time for trivial things." She was getting impatient.

"No, you do not listen. This is important, trust me. You must let me finish," Muirnen said getting a little angry.

"Alright. Go on," the voice responded after a

moment's silence.

"As he was leaving I caught a good look at his face. He looked oddly familiar but I could not place where I had seen him before. Upon further research I found his name to be Demeter. Still I could not think of where I had seen his face. Then, when I returned to the inn and looked upon Jerriney's face again, it came to me. I had not seen this man in my life, but I could see him in Jerriney. Mother, I believe this monk is of her mortal blood."

"This is significant information indeed. Find out where the monk was going and find out who his relatives are. Question Jerriney about him. Your father still refuses to tell me the name of the girl's mother." The voice left him then and he returned to the inn.

"The scrolls mentioned a dragon in the Southern Promoka Mountains that might help us. I think it's best if we head north-east and follow Firetongue Lake. We may get lost traveling through the dense forest. The third option would be to go back south towards Kale and then on to Durma, but that would add another several days of travel," Ron explained to the company as they got ready to leave.

"I agree with you Ron," Drust said. "We should follow the lake. Plus, with the forest being right by the lake, many deer and other animals will come often to drink. We can replenish our meat supplies if we run into any."

"Then we will take that route," Jerriney said as she buckled her sword to her side.

"I dislike water," Nerezzan told Jerriney as he walked up to her.

"It's okay." She laughed. "You don't need to go anywhere near the water." She smiled at him.

"Are you ready Muirnen?" Ron asked him. He had been rather quiet the past couple days.

"Yes, sir. I am quite ready." Muirnen smiled at him.

"Alright let's head out. We've got a long journey ahead of us." Ron led the way out of the inn to their horses in the stable. Before Jerriney went in Ron pulled her back.

"Jerri," Ron said in a hushed voice. "I want you to be careful of Muirnen. He's been way too quiet lately and, if you haven't noticed, he avoids questions about himself and where he came from. Nerezzan also told me he snuck out last night while we were all asleep. Do not put your trust in him."

121

"He seems so nice though. It must be some sort of façade. I'll keep an eye one him. What about Drust? Can I trust him?" Jerriney hoped she could. She had grown quite fond of him.

"Yes, I do believe he is just as he seems, a young man yearning for adventure. If you come to suspect Muirnen of something fiendish I would trust Drust to help you deal with it."

"I will do that. Thank you, Ron." They continued on to retrieve their horses and headed out for Durma.

It was the end of the fourth day of travel and they had one more day until they reached Durma. They had camped down for the night and were sitting around the fire.

"It looks like we could use a little more firewood. I'll go get some," Ron said as he stood up. "Drust, would you come and help me?"

"Sure thing Ron." The two of them went into the forest to gather wood leaving Jerriney, Muirnen, and Nerezzan alone.

"So I've been wondering," Muirnen started, "how did you get your hair so white?" he asked Jerriney.

"I was born with it white." She was poking at the

dwindling fire and, upon mention of her hair, began twirling a strand on her finger.

"Did one of your parents have naturally white hair or something?"

"I don't think so. Well I wouldn't know. I've never met them." Jerriney looked at Muirnen. *"What is he getting at?"* she thought to herself.

"Be careful what you tell him," Nerezzan suddenly stated.

"And your eyes—they're all colored in. How is that possible?" Muirnen already knew these answers but he wanted to see how much she actually knew about herself and her family.

"Once again, I was born that way. I've never seen someone like me, with no pupils." She went back to messing with the fire.

"So Ron is your foster father right?" Muirnen kept questioning her.

"Yea I guess he'd be called that. We're closer than that though." Jerriney smiled at all the good times she had with Ron.

"So do you have any blood relatives around?"

"Don't give him any names," Nerezzan told Jerriney. She nodded mostly at Nerezzan but also to Muirnen's question.

"I have an aunt and an uncle, but they went on a long vacation," Jerriney answered Muirnen. *"A ten-year vacation."* she added to herself.

"You didn't go with them?" Muirnen asked, unconvinced.

"No. It was sort of a wedding anniversary vacation. I wanted to let them have some alone time," Jerriney lied. Normally she would never think of lying but she thought Muirnen was asking these questions for the wrong reasons.

"What do you know about that monk Dem—" Muirnen was cut off by Drust's arrival.

"Hey, is Ron not back yet?" Drust asked after he put an armful of wood on the fire.

"No, he hasn't returned yet. Why?" Jerriney asked.

"He was ahead of me. He should have been here a couple minutes ago," Drust said.

"What do you—"

"Shh!" Drust silenced Jerriney and ducked. He looked out into the darkness. "Did you guys hear a twig crack?" He whispered. They were all quiet, looking around. Drust had his hand on the hilt of his sword.

"It must have been an animal rummaging about." Muirnen broke the silence.

They relaxed a little, except for Drust. He sat down

but he was still alert. They were still for moments following. Jerriney was watching the fire climb as it devoured the new wood. Muirnen had pulled his hood up over his head and Nerezzan was sleeping in the basket Ron made.

Again there was a noise—a shuffling in the bushes behind Jerriney. They all lifted their heads and stiffened. Suddenly they heard someone yell "Jerriney!" followed by the twang of the releasing of an arrow. Jerriney snapped her head around. She saw Ron on the ground but could not evaluate anything more as a burly man came rushing at her. Before she could react Drust was in front of her. He tackled a man who was twice as big as him. Another one came out of the bushes. This time Jerriney was ready and had her sword drawn before he got to her. This man was scrawny and smaller than Jerriney so she knocked him out swiftly. She looked around and saw Muirnen battling another while Drust was still rustling with the first thug. They looked like they had a handle on things so she went to Ron. He had an arrow protruding from his chest. Blood had soaked through his shirt and was starting a pool on the ground.

She knelt beside him. "Ron?"

"Jerriney I, I'm sorry. It—" Ron was interrupted by

his own coughing. "The arrow would have hit you if I hadn't jumped in front of it. He was aiming at you." He managed to say in a weak voice.

"It's okay Ron," she said as she lifted his head into her lap and started crying. "It's gonna be okay. We'll get you to D-Durma and, and we'll find you a doctor and—"

"No, Jerri, I'm done. I won't make it through the night. You must go on without me." Ron lifted his hand to her cheek.

"No! I can't! I won't let you die! Ron, please, I need you. You're my only family. I don't want to be alone." Jerriney sobbed.

"You will never be alone, Jerri. Your father will always look after you." He smiled at her. His hand fell to the ground and his eyes slowly rolled in the back of his head.

"Ron! No, please!" Jerriney hugged him closer. Around her Muirnen was now helping Drust with the huge man. He had bested the one that first came at him and Drust was still struggling with his adversary so he went and helped him. Jerriney could barely hear the clang of metal on metal or smell the mix of sweat and blood. Everything was unreal now as she held on to the man who had been her father and best friend for the

126

past ten years. In the time span of two weeks she had lost not only her aunt and uncle, but also the two people who had raised her for most of her life and whom she saw as her mother and father.

It seemed like an eternity until she felt Drust pick her up. She thought she heard him say something like, "We need to move away from the bodies. We should probably go into town. Bring him with us. We'll bury him in the morning," but she didn't know for sure. She didn't even know if it was Drust who was holding her. The last thing she remembered before she blacked out was someone putting her on a horse.

✝ Chapter Thirteen ✝

The sun shining through the window woke Jerriney. As she regained her senses she realized she was in a bed. She sat up and looked around. There was a young man sitting in a chair looking out the window that she did not recognize.

"Who are you?" Jerriney asked the stranger.

"Jerriney! You're awake! You've been asleep for a whole day!" He rushed to the side of the bed.

"I was sleeping for a whole d—" she stopped herself. "Wait a minute. Who are you?" Jerriney asked for the second time.

"You don't recognize me?" The man held out his arms and turned a full circle. Jerriney just looked at him, waiting for him to explain.

"It's me." The familiar voice filled her mind. It was then that Jerriney finally took a better look at him and stopped at his eyes. They were a familiar bright blue.

"Nerezzan?!" she exclaimed.

"Yes! Except in this form I am called Rhonwen."

128

He bowed at Jerriney as if it was the first time meeting her.

"But you're a big, fluffy, black cat!"

"No, no," Rhonwen chuckled. "That is just one of my forms. I am a Shifter. I can turn into any breathing thing I wish. I have just been in cat form for many years," he explained to her.

"I thought you were a just a talking cat. Where are the others?" Jerriney asked.

"Drust and Muirnen went out on an errand. When you passed out during the attack, I transformed to help clean things up and take care of you. I have already explained myself to the others." He sat down on the bed. "It was necessary that I kept my true identity a secret. I could not watch you as well in human form without interfering."

"What do you mean? Loreen gave you to me. Does she know what you are?" Jerriney flung her legs to the side scooted to the side of the bed to sit by him.

"Yes, Loreen knows. A long time ago she took me in after I had been almost beaten to death by some mages using forbidden magic. Once I had regained my health I sensed you. You see, Jerriney, you are a part of something much bigger than you think. Those blue stones you have are powerful and you are not just a special looking human. If I had come to you in human form and lived with you as a human I would not have been able to keep this information from you for so long. We would have formed a stronger bond and I wouldn't have been able to keep *anything* from you. By not telling you what I'm about to tell you now, your life has been on the path that is vital to your journey." Rhonwen paused to look at her and see how she was taking all this. She looked calm so he continued.

"First off, you are not full-blood human."

"What do you mean?" Jerriney asked. She was a little confused, but felt like deep down she always knew this.

"You have never known the identity of your parents. The only family you know of is John and Tesa, correct?" Rhonwen was taking it slow since he knew this would be a lot to take in.

"Well, yea."

"Before I go on you must promise me something." He looked into her pure, emerald eyes.

"What is it?" Jerriney replied.

"You must promise not tell any of this this information about your family to anyone, especially Muirnen. He is not who he says he is."

"I promise. I will keep this between you and me."

She wondered if she was finally going to know who her parents were.

"Good. Your mother's name is Raleigh Criterious. She is John's sister. She is also the sister of a monk you tried to see, Demeter Criterious. Your father is Baldemor Dahkni. He is The High God of War." Rhonwen let this settle.

"Wait. You mean to say I am half-god?" She looked at him with eyes wide open.

"That is exactly what I mean to say. That is why your hair is silvery white and your eyes are a beautiful emerald with no pupils. It is also the reason for a number of other things, including your destiny."

"Wait, can we go back to the fact that my father is a god!" Jerriney wondered if she might get to meet him someday.

"We can talk about that on another day. Right now we do not have time. You need to know what you are dealing with and realize how much more important your goal is." Rhonwen looked at her sternly.

"Alright. I suppose I can wait," she said, a little disappointed. Rhonwen got up and walked to the window.

"Those blue stones your aunt and uncle sent you are actually regular stones, but the reason they are blue is because they are magicked. A long time ago, a mage put a very strong spell on them, which is keeping five High Dragons' souls in them, one in each. He intended to capture all twelve of the High Dragons, who are the leaders of dragons all over the world, to use their power for his own use, which was to rule the world. He has long since died, but there is a man who has learned of these stones and wants to continue what the mage started." He took his eyes from the bustle of daily life in Durma back to Jerriney.

"Why didn't Loreen know this? She said they were Prometheans." Jerriney could not believe that Loreen made a mistake.

"She knows of this story, but these days it is not brought up very often where the story of the Stone Wielders is widely popular for retelling to children. Plus, Prometheans and these stones look virtually the same," Rhonwen answered her.

"How did he get their souls then? I thought the High Dragons could not be killed by anything except another dragon?"

"Ah, see the mage didn't kill them. He sucked their souls out with Dark Magic, thus making their physical body decay. How he subdued them to be able to do this, I do not know."

"So, what am I supposed to do to stop this mage?" Jerriney joined him by the window.

"You must journey to the Promoka Mountains and find the dragon that dwells in a cave to the south. I cannot tell you how to defeat the man, but this dragon should be able to help you."

Drust and Muirnen walked in the room.

"Jerriney!" Drust exclaimed as he ran towards her, pushing Rhonwen to the side. He embraced her in a hug and kissed her on the cheek. Jerriney stood there stunned.

"You were out for a whole day! I thought you were never going to wake!" Drust held her at arm's length. "How are you?"

Muirnen, who was leaning against the wall, rolled his eyes.

"I'm fine, Drust, thank you. Why was I sleeping for a whole day?" Jerriney asked.

"Well after we were ambushed you wouldn't let go of ..." Drust trailed off. He did not want to upset Jerriney by saying his name.

"What? Wait. Ron! Where's Ron! Is he okay?" Jerriney suddenly remembered what happened the previous night.

"I'm sorry Jerriney, he died in your arms. That's

why you slept for a day. Your body and mind were in shock," Drust answered her. Jerriney slumped onto the bed. Tears started falling from her eyes.

"Muirnen and I went out to dig a hole. We can go and bury him now," Drust said softly as he held her.

They stood up to leave. Drust looked at Rhonwen and suddenly reached for his dagger. "Hold it there!" he yelled. Then upon remembering who Rhonwen was, blushed and relaxed his arms.

"Geez Nerezzan, I'm still not used to your human form. I didn't even see you when I walked in. I was so focused on Jerri I thought you were a thief!"

Rhonwen chuckled. "It's okay Drust, I'm not quite used to it myself. I saw my reflection in the window this morning and it startled me. Boy did I feel silly. And remember, in this form I'm called Rhonwen." He smiled at the young man. "Let us give Ron a proper burial."

𝕿hey didn't speak much on the way back to the inn. Once they were in their room and starting to relax a little they started to talk.

"We searched the bodies to try and find who ambushed us. We didn't find much on them. But the

134

one really big guy had this note," Drust said as he handed Jerriney a piece of paper. She took the note from him.

It read:

Hair: long, silvery white
Eyes: Green, no pupils
Height: taller than average

She may be with other people. Kill them. Get the stones then kill her. If she does not give you the stones and you cannot take them from her, bring her alive to me in Durma. If you mess this one up, I WILL have your heads.
- D.C.

"Have you all read this?" Jerriney asked the group. They nodded in response. "It's a description of me." She handed the note back to Drust.

"That's what we thought. I mean, I doubt there is any other person alive with your unique qualities and happen to carry blue stones with them," Drust pointed out. They all chuckled a little at that although it did not last long. Their thoughts were still on Ron.

"So what should we do about this?" Jerriney asked them.

"I propose we keep moving as quickly as we can. I expect whoever this D.C. is will have more people to send after us. From the note it seems he isn't one to give up easily," Muirnen said.

"That's another matter we need to find out. Who D.C. is," said Rhonwen.

"I don't know anyone with those initials," Jerriney replied.

"Dashelgar Crainten," Drust responded. "I heard two customers at the blacksmith talking about some ambush on the Amensdale Ocean. The captain's name was Dashlegar Crainten. He was the only one to survive. There were also some of the king's men onboard." He looked from Rhonwen to Jerriney.

"We know of the ambush," Rhonwen commented. "But we did not know the name of the captain. If he is behind *this* ambush than the attack on the ocean might have been more than just an ambush."

"Could this Dashlegar be the man in the prophecy that you told me about in the forest before Loreen told me what the stones were?" Jerriney queried the group.

"I have a feeling it is. When I heard Drust speak his name a feeling of foreboding was aroused deep inside me. I advise we be very careful when dealing with him. If he truly is the man the prophecy spoke of than he is very powerful and may be familiar with Dark Magic," Rhonwen responded. Then, looking at Jerriney, he quickly added, "Have you felt anything from the stones? Any sort of power drawing you to them or an unexplainable stirring inside?"

"No, I don't think so. I thought I felt something strange when we were ambushed. It was a feeling I'm not familiar with. I figured it was just shock from seeing Ron shot," Jerriney replied.

"Hmm. We can't be sure what that was then. Maybe if you tried reaching out to the stones," Rhonwen thought aloud.

"Since you have the blood of a god in you, you have your own magic. You have already seen it. You have used it when you brought injured animals that Liz declared beyond repair but you nursed them back to health. You also used your magic in the garden. Remember how surprised and delighted Liz was when you got her flowers to blossom two or three more heads than she ever could? You never physically did anything

137

different than everyone else but you unintentionally spread magic into the animals and plants. If you can grasp a hold of this power, find it deep inside you, then you can add that to the power from the stones and overcome any obstacle. I say this to you through your mind because Muirnen is present. Do not forget, he cannot know of this."

While Rhonwen telepathically spoke to Jerriney, Drust and Muirnen suggested ways for her to try and channel the power of the stones. She looked back and forth from the two young men while listening to Rhonwen. Jerriney tried to look like she was listening to Drust and Muirnen but she didn't catch a word of what they said as a result of Rhonwen's thoughts resounding in her head. When Rhonwen finished speaking to her she looked at him and nodded slightly, acknowledging what he said.

"Do you think you could tap into the stones' powers Jerri?" She heard Drust ask.

"I'm sure if I concentrate and look deep inside I can find a way to use the stones powers." She hoped she didn't look too confused to Drust and Muirnen and that her answer was somewhat what they were looking for.

"Alright, I think it's time we hit the hay and get a

good night's rest before we head off to the Promoka Mountains in the morning. There aren't any towns along the way so this will be the last we get to stay in nice beds with a roof above our heads and walls keeping us safe," Rhonwen suggested.

"Oh wait!" Drust said. "I found this on one of the men's body. It looks like a page ripped out of a book. I can't read it though. I can hardly read our own language and this is something I've never seen before."

Muirnen grabbed the page before Rhonwen or Jerriney could get it. He read it silently to himself. "It is a page from an ancient tome that was banned a long time ago, before the current king. It tells how a warlock of long ago captured some of the High Dragons and using Dark Magic he imprisoned their souls in magicked stones so he could use their power himself. He almost got all of them. In fact only three of the High Dragons escaped from him. They fled Amensdale and haven't been seen since. All the other dragons have gone into hiding as well and they have lost all trust in humans." Muirnen handed the page to Rhonwen.

"Ah yes. I remember that story. The first dragon soul he extracted was one who loved him dearly. She would do anything for him. Then he started looking up Dark Magic and practicing it. She didn't have a clue.

Her judgment was clouded by love and trust," Rhonwen told them.

"How many High Dragons did you say there are?" Jerriney asked.

"There are twelve. Nine of their souls are trapped in stones."

"Jerri has six stones," Drust said. "Does she have some of the stones with dragon souls in them?"

"I have read in a different book that the warlock lost five of the stones in battle, but he still had four," Muirnen said.

"I believe Jerriney does carry the rest of the High Dragons' souls. That is why people have tried to kill her," Rhonwen added.

"But that would make thirteen stones total. I thought there were only twelve," noted Drust.

Jerriney took out her pouch and poured the contents onto her hand. Six blue stones shone brilliantly in the light. One was slightly smaller than the others and a lighter shade of blue. She picked it up.

"This one is a dragon tear," Jerriney told Drust.

"How is that possible?" Drust queried.

Rhonwen grinned. "Jerri found it in the mud while hunting. It must have fallen from a dying dragon flying overhead years ago."

"Then how did she happen upon it if it was years ago? Would someone else hunting not have found it?" Muirnen asked.

"It must have been stomped in the ground by deer and other animals and then pulled back up by nesting animals and rain and wind."

"How did it not seep into the soil? Did it get stuck in that stone?" Drust continued, still confused how something liquid could now be what seemed like a stone.

"No, it's not a stone at all," Jerriney told him. "It's pure dragon magic. When I showed it to a wise lady back in my home town she said when it fell from the sky, elements in the air had some kind of chemical reaction with the magic in the tear and formed a case around it." Jerriney put the stones back into the pouch.

"It is getting late. We can talk more about this later if need be. Let us get some sleep for the road ahead," Rhonwen said. They all nodded their agreements and were soon fast asleep.

They were ready to leave for the Promoka Mountains bright and early the next morning. Jerriney took her time packing, carefully folding her extra set of clothes. It would be some time before they had such nice accommodations and she wanted to absorb as much of it as she could. They would stop at Rohalla Lake and camp by the water to rest for a night. They could refill their water skins there and maybe catch some more animals that came to drink to re-stock their meat supply. They had also heard that it was the best lake on a hot day. It was always the perfect temperature for cooling down.

It took them about three days to get to the lake. While they traveled, Rhonwen told Jerriney that her duty now was to return the High Dragons' souls to the dragons. He said she should ask the dragon mentioned in Demeter's writings for help. Jerriney still could not believe that her destiny was so important to the survival of Amensdale and that she had the blood of a god! This was another thing she spoke to Rhonwen about while they traveled.

"Before Ron died," he said. *"Your father will always watch over you." Do you think he meant my actual father?"* Jerriney asked Rhonwen, remembering to speak through their minds so Muirnen could not hear.

"I imagine he did. I do not know whether or not anyone knew who your real parents were. I bet John and Tesa knew and made sure Ron and Liz knew too

before they left for that mission."

"*I wonder why no one told me,*" Jerriney said, this time to herself.

𝕿hey got to the lake when the sun was still up and since it was a hot day they decided to take a swim to relax and cool off. They stayed in the water until the sun started to set and it began to cool down. Rhonwen got the fire going and Drust started making soup with some rabbits he caught while looking for firewood. Muirnen went to bed early. Rhonwen wanted to go sit by the water for a while before he settled down for the night. He said it had been a while since he had the chance to admire the lake life since he had been a cat for so many years. Drust and Jerriney were left around the fire.

"So, you told us you lost your parents in a fire, but I don't really know anything else about you," Jerriney said to Drust.

"Well, what would you like to know?" Drust looked at her, his blue eyes reflecting the stars in the sky.

"Where did you live when you were a child? I

143

mean, before your parents passed away."

"Actually, we lived in Morga." Drust smiled at Jerriney.

"What? You mean you lived in the villages outside, right?" Jerriney could not believe that he came from a wealthy family, as they were the only ones allowed to live inside the city's walls.

"Nope. We lived *in* Morga. Not far from the king's castle actually. We could often see him coming and going with his crowd of escorts." Drust picked up a twig that missed the fire and snapped it in two.

"So, you mean your family was rich? Why did you have to go live with a blacksmith then? Surely you had people around you willing to take you in." Jerriney moved closer to Drust, intrigued in his mysterious background.

"Oh I had plenty of options. We had butlers and maids who all offered to integrate me into their family. I *chose* to go to the blacksmith. I was ten so I was old enough to work. I wasn't the strongest at the time, but it didn't take long for the muscles to kick in." Drust was still picking up twigs from the fire and breaking them. He had never told his life story to anyone. People had tried to get him to open up before but he was afraid to let anyone in and letting them get close to him. He was

144

afraid to lose those he loved again so he just chose not to let others have a chance to care about him. But with Jerriney, Drust suddenly wanted, no needed, to open up to her. He wasn't sure why.

"Why did you choose that kind of life? You could have had anything in the world, but instead you just have yourself. Why didn't you want to continue living in Morga where people could love and care for you?" Jerriney felt sadness for Drust. For the boy who lost his parents and then purposely lost everything else. She did not understand how *anyone* could choose that for themselves.

"I took my parents' death hard. I didn't want any reminders of them. I was also was bored with the wealthy life. You see, when you have all the coin you need and plenty to spare, you don't get the luxury of really living. I had all the toys I wanted, got all the treats and desserts I asked for, if I didn't like a butler or a maid my parents would have them gone before I even asked of it." Drust had run out of twigs now and was just staring into the fire. "I wanted to see what it was like to have a life that I actually earned. I had often traveled to the city walls and just watched the kids my age play with toys they had made themselves. They seemed so much happier then I was. That was all I

145

wanted." He looked at Jerriney. They were both silent for a moment.

"Did you get that?" Jerriney quietly asked.

Drust laughed and looked at his hands. "No. I worked the rest of my life. I never had time to play and make friends, but I was happy. Happiest I'd ever been." He looked back and Jerriney. "Until I met you."

More silence.

Jerriney blushed and looked at the fire. She cleared her throat. "Um, it's getting late. I think I hear Rhonwen coming back. We should get to sleep." She peeked a glance at Drust and saw him smiling at her. She blushed again and got up.

"I'm a bit tired too," Drust said. "Good night Jerriney."

𝔚︎hen they had everything packed up in the morning they took one last swim in the lake and continued on towards the mountains. They had traveled all day, so around sunset they decided to make camp near the foot of a mountain and rest for the remainder of the day and that night.

"I noticed there are a lot of caves in these mountains," Jerriney said. "Should we sleep in one of those?"

"I don't think that would be safe," Rhonwen replied. "We don't know what animals or people are around here. We wouldn't want to intrude on something that might be hostile."

"He makes a good point. I think it's wise if we stay here, at the foot of the mountain," Muirnen commented.

"I think it would be interesting to sleep in a cave," Drust said. The others just looked at him.

"What? I just think it would be fun to explore them," he explained.

"More like he's just agreeing with Jerriney to get on her good side," Muirnen muttered under his breath, making Jerriney chuckle.

"No really! I've never been in a cave," Drust argued. Then he added in a slightly defeated voice, "I just thought it would be fun."

Once they finished eating and the sun had set they bedded down for the night. Jerriney lay in her blankets for a while looking at the stars. There was so much up there. She sometimes wondered if there were other people out there. Then she remembered what Rhonwen had told her. Her father was a god. There are gods out there. Did they maybe live somewhere way up in the sky? She fell asleep thinking about what the gods looked like and what it would be like to have been raised with them instead of with mortals.

"𝕷ook at this one." Jerriney stirred from her sleep to hear a raspy voice. She didn't move in fear of what would happen, instead she just listened.

"This female's got white hair, but she's not an old one," it said.

"You think she's got a magical artifact that makes her face stay young?" Jerriney heard another voice pipe in. This one was a deep bass.

"Ooo maybe she has something shiny!" A third voice exclaimed in a high pitch. She found this one rather annoying.

Jerriney focused her hearing on her surroundings. There were several of whatever it was that had invaded their camp. They were rummaging through their things. Whatever creatures they were, they didn't smell good. She remembered reading something when she was younger. Goblins liked shiny things. They also had poor hygiene.

She slowly opened one of her eyes. There was a goblin admiring himself in the shine of her sword. He suddenly noticed she was peeking at him.

"Oi! This 'un's awake!" he said to his fellow goblins.

"Grab her!" Jerriney heard one of them exclaimed as he rushed at her.

"Drust!" Jerriney yelled as loud as she could as she jumped to her feet and kicked a pot to wake him just before the goblin grabbed her.

Drust awoke as the pot collided into his stomach and saw Jerriney struggling. He shouted for her and dived at his sword but another goblin was behind him and grabbed his arm before he got to it.

"Let her go!" Drust yelled.

"The others are stirring! Grab them before they can do anything," said the goblin that had a hold of Drust, ignoring his comment.

Jerriney could see now that there were at least twelve goblins. They didn't have a chance against them. These guys were bigger than what she had learned about them in books.

"What do you want?" Jerriney shouted as she pulled against the goblin's hold.

"They don't want anything, Jerri. These are cave goblins," Rhonwen explained as calmly as he could. A pair of goblins grabbed him out of his sleeping sack. "They raid anyone they stumble upon for shiny things, and then they kill them and leave with what they want."

"And you guys don't have much time to live!" Said a particularly large, ugly goblin that was covered in an assortment of jewelry and warts. "You don't have very many things with you so it didn't take us long to find what we wanted."

"Let's kill the pretty one first!" The goblin holding Jerriney said as he pulled out a dagger. "It looks like the one with the dirty, yellow hair over there seems to have a liking for her." He waved the rusty dagger towards Drust. "I wanna see his face as I bleed the life out of her."

Suddenly a hooded figure appeared behind him with a knife pressed against his leathery dark green throat. "You'll be doing no such thing," the stranger whispered in the goblin's pierced ear as he slit his throat. Then the hooded figure disappeared into thin air.

"Did you see that?!" asked one of the smaller goblins. "He just killed him and then poofed into nothing!"

The rest of the band started to get restless and were looking all over for this mysterious killer.

"Calm down!" the large goblin said. "Be on you guard, but do not panic! That's just what the cloaked creature wants. We start seeing shadows and then accidentally hit one of our own! Watc—" Blood spurted out of his mouth as he tried to finish speaking. He clenched his stomach and looked down. Dark, red liquid flowed from between his fingers.

Suddenly, the camp was filled with screaming goblins trying to flee as hooded black figures began slaying them, disappearing into a dark mist before the goblins hit the ground.

Jerriney thought the scene went by way too fast. It was merely seconds before most of the goblins lay dead around the camp. The last one was running off towards the caves in the mountains. She then noticed there were four cloaked figures standing in the middle of their camp.

✝ Chapter Fourteen ✝

Drust unsheathed his sword and was about to rush the strangers.

"Do not be afraid. We are friends," said the one closest to them as he held out a hand, palm facing forward. He appeared to be the leader of the group.

"My name is Draxx." He uncloaked his head revealing shoulder-length curly black hair. He beckoned the others to do the same. "This is Nazema," he continued as a young woman stepped forward from his left side as he said her name. She had luxurious, golden hair and looked like she was eighteen. She curtsied to Jerriney's group.

"Nazema is unable to speak so unfortunately she cannot give you her welcome, but I'm sure she is pleased to meet you." Draxx put a gentle arm around her waist and smiled at Nazema. "This man on my left is Nicodemus."

"Hello friends." He stepped forward and vigorously shook Drust's hand, his unusually long white eyebrows bobbing from the force. "You may call me Nic," he said as joined the rest.

"And here on my right is Melanthious."

"Pleasure to meet you," the man said as he slightly bowed, traces of grey were starting to show on the top of his hair.

"We were on our way home when we smelt goblin stench. We have been trying to rid this area of those cave dwellers for quite some time. We are glad that they had not killed you," Draxx said as he bent down to examine one of the goblin's daggers. "So many times we have come upon dead travelers fallen victim to these vile creatures, so when we say it is a pleasure to meet you, we say it with all sincerity." He stood back up. "It is nice to have company outside of our own every once in a while." Draxx smiled.

Jerriney and her group where so shocked by what had just happened, they did not know how to respond. The cloaked strangers seemed friendly enough, but no one in her group could find their voice, so they ended up staring wide-eyed.

"And who might you be?" Draxx tried.

"Excuse our silence," Rhonwen finally spoke. "We are not used to almost being killed by goblins, first thing in the morning, and saved by strangers before we're even fully awake."

153

"But we thank you for your speedy elimination of the goblins," Drust added.

"I am Jerriney," she stepped forward, her hair shimmering silver in the morning light. "This is Drust, Muirnen, and Rhonwen." She introduced each as she gestured to them accordingly. "We were headed towards the Southern Promoka Mountains and were just resting here for the night. May I ask how you killed those goblins so swiftly?"

"Ah, well I do believe your friend Rhonwen could answer your question." Draxx grinned at him.

"Rhonwen?" Jerriney looked at him puzzled. "You know these people?"

"Well, not personally, but I do know what they are, which in turn, can answer your question," Rhonwen told Jerriney. "I have already explained to you that I am a Shifter. These people here are just like me, except they have been alive quite a bit longer than I. One even came into existence centuries before I was born, which also makes them ..." He paused a while to think of the correct way to explain, "like a different breed of Shifters. I suppose that would be easy for you to understand."

"How are they different than you?" Muirnen asked.

"They are much more powerful and their abilities

are not as limited as mine." Rhonwen began to collect his things, as did the others. "When we shift into something we have to know every single detail from the feeling of the fur or skin to the pattern of spots or stripes. Even eating habits and movements, down to the bone structure, where the heart is placed and all the other organs. Every detail, even the tiniest ones you can't see with the naked eye or without magic, we have to make sure is perfect." He secured his belongings, and then hoisted himself onto his horse. The others followed suit.

"Now it doesn't always have to be completely perfect, but if we want to hide well from people who know how to recognize a Shifter, then we have to make sure everything is in its proper place. If one just wanted to prance around for a while as a young colt than all that is needed are the basics. The way we get this information is very special. Once we come upon the creature we wish to shift into, we have to transform into our true form and literally go into the creature and see its life and the way it functions hands-on. Then—"

"What is your true form?" Jerriney interrupted, her emerald eyes sparkling with curiosity.

Nicodemus answered as he and his fellow Shifters walked along the horses, "Our true form is sort-of what humans think spirits look like, but more visible. We all have a unique true form that changes with our age and personality, but they all are sort-of liquid looking. It is quite hard to describe. Not many have seen us in our true form, and that is how it has to stay as we are most vulnerable in it for reasons we have not found out."

Rhonwen nodded then continued, "Once we have learned all we need, we leave the body exactly how we found it. While this whole process goes on the creature knows nothing of us, unless we tell it, and we do not interfere in any way. The creature goes through its daily life just as if we were not there. Now, the way we are different is this is the way my generation of Shifters get information. The ones born way before us, before this land was settled, found a way to get all this from just a footprint or a follicle of hair. It is a magic that has been lost due to humans, goblins, trolls, and many other creatures hunting us down. We are a peaceful race so not many of us survived. Most who knew our secrets were slaughtered. Here, we have what may be the last known survivors, who have our race's greatest secrets, which includes the swiftest and most painless way to eliminate enemies." Rhonwen turned to the ancient Shifters. "I am very honored to meet you." He stopped his horse and gracefully bowed his head to the four.

✝ Chapter Fifteen ✝

The eight of them continued on towards the Southern Promoka Mountains. Jerriney said they could make room on the horses for the Shifters to ride, but they said they could keep up just fine on foot. Rhonwen asked many questions of his fellow Shifters. He seemed like a cat with too many mice to chase, excited to be in the presence of these old Shifters, but so full of questions and things he wanted to learn, that he often stumbled over his words and interrupted the Shifters with new queries. Then Nicodemus replied to one of Rhonwen's questions with an answer that made him ponder deeply.

Draxx took this break to speak to Jerriney. "You told us you were heading to the Southern Promoka Mountains but you did not speak of what you were searching for. May I ask what it is you seek?"

Jerriney thought these Shifters were trust-worthy people so she decided to be fully honest with them. "Well it's sort of a long story. Maybe later we can tell you the whole version, but right now we are searching for the dragon that we heard was taking refuge in a cave in the southern mountains. We need some important information from it."

"Really? Someone knows of the dragon here? Who told you?" the usually silent Melanthious asked.

"A monk in Duvok, called Demeter, wrote of it in one of his prophecies. It was a while ago so I hope it still resides around here." Jerriney was truly quite worried that something might have happened to the dragon. She didn't know where she would go next if it had died of old age or someone had hunted and killed it.

"You don't think they mean—"

"Sully!" Nic said with much enthusiasm as he interrupted Melanthious.

"Excuse me?" Rhonwen looked at Draxx, confused.

Nazema smiled, her brown eyes glistening.

Draxx chuckled. "We are quite acquainted with the dragon you speak of. We call her Sully because her real name is far too complex to pronounce. When you meet her you will hear her say it though."

"So you mean you guys actually know a dragon?" Jerriney asked them.

"Oh yes! Sully is quite a companion to fly with!" Nicodemus was beaming with happiness at the thought of this dragon.

"Nic seems to be quite fond of this Sully," Muirnen observed.

"Indeed. Nic and Sully spend a lot of time together. I think it has something to do with the closeness of their age." He looked at Nic and grinned, then he put a hand to the side of his mouth and added, "Both of them are starting to go loopy."

The group laughed in unison.

As they continued towards the southern mountains the Shifters told stories of the times they spent with Sully. They were so distracted by the joyful memories, they didn't notice that the sun was almost fully set.

"We should probably stop and camp here for the night," Draxx suggested.

Once the camp was set, Jerriney had a question for the newfound Shifters, it had been pressing on her mind for quite some time.

"What exactly are you guys doing out here?" she asked Draxx.

"You do not know the story of the Shifters in this part of the world?" Draxx asked in bewilderment.

"What do you mean?" Confusion rang in Jerriney's voice.

"You travel with a Shifter yet you do not know

anything of us?" Melanthious asked.

"That would be my fault," Rhonwen said. "I just recently told her that I was a Shifter. For many years I have been a cat, subtly helping her get to this point in time. Years ago, I spoke with my former owner and we agreed that I should be given as a gift to her in order that she would one day take on this journey. I am to help inform her in this new world of magic and dragons that she is not used to. All she knows of us is what was told when we met you. I intended on telling her more but we have been busy with more pressing matters."

"I see. Well then, before we sleep we can tell you why Shifters are not seen anymore," Draxx told Jerriney. "We are here in the mountains because we are hiding."

"Hiding? From what?" Jerriney couldn't think of why such powerful creatures would be hiding. *"Maybe it's sort of like why dragons are hiding."* she thought to herself.

"We are hiding from humans," Melanthious stated, his amber eyes glowing orange in the firelight.

"Have you ever heard of Wraiths, Jerriney?" Nicodemus asked her.

"I have heard them mentioned. Aren't they evil creatures?" Jerriney replied as she sat on the soft dirt.

"Not at all. They were just misunderstood. The first Shifters that came here were called Wraiths," Draxx explained.

"But aren't Shifters a peaceful race? I heard that Wraiths burnt up towns mercilessly. Many people died; women and children as well as men." Jerriney did not understand.

"We *are* a peaceful race," Rhonwen said. "We would never kill mercilessly. We were trying to save the human race, which we did, by burning what was necessary."

Jerriney looked very confused.

"Let us start at the beginning," Draxx said. "Shifters came to this land for one reason—to stop a pestilence that would have eventually spread all over the world, killing not only humans but most of the animals as well." He added a log to the fire. "Some Shifters have prophetic visions, sort of like your monks in their Abbeys. They had seen what this pestilence could do and decided to take it into their own hands to prevent the vision from coming true. They came to this land and burned all that had been infected with this horrible virus."

"Why didn't you just warn the king? He could have had the sick people quarantined." Jerriney thought

161

burning everything was a little over the top.

"Because the king would not have listened to us," Draxx continued, "and if he did, we knew he would try to do something like what you mentioned and that would not have worked. The pestilence was caused by a fungus that started growing on older buildings. It was in some kind of material people used hundreds of years ago to keep houses warm. Over time it began to rot and slowly leaked out, infecting anything that breathed. There was no cure and no way to make one. The only way to get rid of it was by fire. We had to burn everything infected by it. Believe me, the first Shifters that came here did not want to be introduced into this land by such a way, but they feared the loss of human kind."

Jerriney pondered this for a little while. "I guess that makes sense, but the Wraiths were lizard-like. You guys look like humans."

"Just like humans have different cultures and wear different clothing, certain Shifters have certain preferred shapes. There is what you may call a lizard culture, where the Shifters look like lizard humanoids. There are some that prefer to appear wolf-like. There are many, many different cultures," Melanthious explained.

"Oh, I see," Jerriney said. "Well I am quite tired. I think we should call it a night." They all agreed and were soon fast asleep—except one.

✝ Chapter Sixteen ✝

Muirnen closed his eyes and listened for the others breathing to slow, signaling that they were finally asleep. Once they were out, he quietly got up and started walking back the way they had come. He had seen a little cave that was hidden from the view of the camp and far enough away that he would not be heard.

"Mother?" he quietly said. The air around him thickened. A fog crept through the small cave making swirls in the dirt. A woman's head and torso formed out of the fog.

"What is it, child?" his mother answered quite sharply. "Why have you taken so long to contact me?"

"I apologize, mother. I could not get away from them for a while," Muirnen explained, taking his hood off.

"Did you find out anything about the monk? Did Jerriney tell you her mother's name?" The goddess aggressively crossed her arms.

"Before I left the Abbey, I found out that the monk

Demeter had gone to see his sister. The elderly monk I questioned would not tell me her name or what town Demeter was heading to. He said he did not trust my motives for questioning him. As for Jerriney, I cannot seem to get to her to talk about her family. Honestly, I do not think she knows her heritage herself," Muirnen told his impatient mother.

"I suppose that is better than nothing. Keep questioning the girl. The Shifter that was living with her might know who her mother is. Question him as well."

"I do not think Rhonwen trusts me, mother. Asking him questions might get me kicked out of the group," he hesitantly said for he did not want to anger her further.

"Find a way!" The angry goddess boomed, her voice ricocheting off the walls of the small cave, attacking Muirnen. He hated when she added magic into her shouts. It always gave him a terrible headache.

"I will do my best, mother." Muirnen bowed as his testy mother's form disappeared into the night. Muirnen quietly crept back into the camp and went to sleep.

The next morning, the Shifters told Jerriney that the dragon's cave was not far and that they would be there by nightfall. They ate breakfast and began their day's journey south.

"While we are traveling, do you mind telling us of your journey thus far?" Melanthious asked Jerriney,

Jerriney looked at Rhonwen for confirmation on whether or not she should tell them.

"You can trust any Shifter Jerriney," Rhonwen assured her. *"But be careful, Muirnen is among us."*

"It all starts back with my aunt and uncle," Jerriney began. "They had given one of the king's messengers a pouch of stones to send to me if any ill befell them. While they were on their way home from a mission their ship was ambushed. The captain, Dashlegar Crainten, claims that the rest of the crew was lost, drowned by the sea or killed by goblins. Upon hearing this, the messenger brought me the pouch of five blue stones. I went to the town elder, Loreen, who claimed they were Prometheans, which are stones soaked in dragons' tears. She told me the story of the Stone Wielders and how they misused the dragons' magic, causing dragons to loose trust in humans. Then she said that it is up to me to return the stones as a sort-of peace offering and get the trust of the dragons back." Jerriney shifted in her saddle.

"So I began my journey. Before I left, Loreen told

me that a monk in Duvok might know the whereabouts of a dragon so we traveled to the Abbey. On our way there, we met Drust in Kale and Muirnen on the way up to Duvok. They chose to join us on our travels. Muirnen, to find a home that suited him, and Drust was at first picking up supplies for his master's blacksmith shop and guiding us through the dangerous streets of Duvok, but then decided to continue to help us. After we found the location of the dragon, we started toward the Promoka Mountains. We were then ambushed by men, who we believe were sent by Dashlegar Crainten.

"After Rhonwen inspected the stones for the first time, he told me that they were not Prometheans, but dragon souls trapped in the stones. My goal now is to return the souls to the dragons, and to make sure the dark mage does not get ahold of them."

"This is a heavy burden that has been put upon such a young girl's shoulders," said Melanthious as he stroked the neck of Jerriney's horse. "Why did you not give someone else the stones to return to the dragons?"

"Yes, it is a heavy burden, but I believe that this is why I was put on this earth. I have lived from house to house, family to family, my whole life. My aunt and uncle who raised me, until I was seven, supposedly died in a sea ambush. Everyone I love has died. I see no other path for me than to save Amensdale from a very dark future," Jerriney explained. "There's nothing else for me. I don't even know who my real parents are," she added, then looked at Rhonwen, realizing that was something she probably should have left out. He was looking at Muirnen for his response to the statement. Muirnen just shrunk deeper into his hood.

"Did I say too much?" Jerriney asked Rhonwen through her mind.

"I do not like the way he reacted to that. You probably should not have said anything regarding your parents. I don't believe he is looking for new home," Rhonwen replied to her in the same manner.

"If you wish it, and if my companions agree with me, we would proudly join you in your quest to bring the souls back to their dragon owners. From the sound of it, you could use our help and protection," Draxx told her. He ran up so he would be even with Jerriney and Rhonwen.

Jerriney was still worried about Muirnen's true reason for joining them so Rhonwen replied in her stead. "We would be honored for you to join us. First, we need to ask this dragon, Sully, what exactly to do with the stones."

Jerriney nodded in agreement.

"We are almost there," Nicodemus stated.

They arrived at the dragon's cave to find it empty. It was fairly large; big enough for the dragon to fit in comfortably along with plenty room for the Shifters.

"She must be hunting," Draxx commented. "Make yourselves comfortable. Sully will let you stay here for the night."

They dismounted their horses and let them graze on the grass outside the cave. Draxx started a fire.

Sully was taking quite a long time to return so they began chatting among themselves.

Nicodemus was telling Drust of the many herbs one could use to make a tincture of Non-blunt which temporarily makes your sword stay sharp, no matter how many hits it takes. Nicodemus thought Drust would be interested since it had to do with swords and he used to work as a blacksmith, but the herbs were ones that either could not be found growing in Amensdale or were very rare. At first Drust was intrigued, but Nic went into every detail of the recipe—where the herbs were found, what other things they could do, and the precise way they needed to be

169

mixed to make the tincture, so Drust found himself staring idly into the fire.

Not far away from Drust and Nicodemus, Jerriney sat with Rhonwen observing the scene.

"Nic reminds me a lot of Loreen," Jerriney said to Rhonwen. He looked over to see Nic enthusiastically explaining to Drust how to harvest the hardy Morrowthin plant, not even noticing that Drust was not paying attention. Rhonwen chuckled.

"Both of them are crazy." He smiled at Jerriney, his eyes, still in the form of a cats, shined in the darkness.

"Speaking of Loreen," Jerriney started, "is she Fae?"

"What?" Rhonwen's expression looked like he thought Jerriney just asked an absurd question. "Are you asking me if Loreen is a fairy?!"

"Well, yea." Jerriney was a little embarrassed. She looked at her feet and scuffed at the dirt. "She knows so much and is so talented that I suspected she knows magic. Am I wrong in my assumption?"

"Yes you are, but do not be embarrassed. Many probably think the same. She is not Fae Folk, but she could talk to them freely if she wanted. Loreen is a most interesting human. She is fully mortal, yet she lives years and years beyond the average life expectancy of a human. She immerses herself in the unknown and magical. She loves to learn new things. She also has the ability to use some magic."

"I did not know mortals could use magic." Jerriney did not realize how much of an amazing woman Loreen must be.

"They can't." Rhonwen smiled at her.

"Then how?" Jerriney was so confused now that she didn't finish her sentence.

"On their own that is. She has been granted certain powers over the years by immortal beings. I believe even the Fairy Queen herself gave a bit of magic to Loreen. She has also found tomes that have incantations of which, if you say over a particular mix of herbs, can grant you certain powers." Rhonwen took a piece of bread out of a bag and took a bite.

"That's incredible. I bet she knows a whole lot more than we believe. I mean, I knew she was very wise and knows a lot more about the world than anyone, but she is probably even wiser than what I thought before!" Jerriney could not wait to see Loreen again. She could learn so much from her.

"Aye, that is true. Loreen is the best ally you can have, and the worst enemy." Rhonwen remembered when Loreen saved him from a band of Dark Users—mages who use Dark Magic. He sure was glad she was on his side that day.

Suddenly there was a loud roar from the mouth of the cave. They all looked at the green dragon that made the ferocious noise. Jerriney knew this must be Sully, but she felt like this dragon did not like the company that was in her cave.

"WHO DARES BRING THE OFFSPRING OF A GOD INTO MY PLACE OF REST?!" Her voice resounded through Jerriney and the rest of the group's heads. Dragons spoke directly to the minds of those they wished to be heard by. Jerriney now knew for sure that this dragon was not happy with them being there.

"Sully! It is us!" Nicodemus said, walking toward her, his long white hair and beard flying behind him from the dragon's huffing. "Please be calm, the girl is our friend."

"You know fairly well the relationship between dragons and gods. You should never have brought her here! I will not have her kind stinking up the place with their lies and deception!" Sully snapped her maw at Nic, smoke coming out of her nostrils.

"What does she mean?" Jerriney said to anyone who could answer her. She did not understand why this dragon, whom she had never met, was accusing her of lying and being deceitful.

"A long time ago, the dragons used to rule this land," Melanthious quickly told Jerriney. "There were thousands of them, and they had immense power. One day, the gods decided to take away some of their power. This started a long war between dragons and the gods. Although it is over, dragons still have a great disliking for the gods and anything that has to do with them."

"Because of them we can be slayed by any puny mortal—a death not worthy of any of my kin! Now there are very few of us, some trapped by magic made from our own stolen power and given to the humans! We used to live in peace! We made no war with any being of this land. We did not deserve this." She growled at Jerriney, the fire reflecting in her eyes making her even more frightening.

"This girl knew nothing of her immortal blood until a few days ago. She did not know of the feud between dragons and gods. She is probably the most peaceful being in this land and she is the only one who can save Amensdale from complete destruction," Rhonwen bravely marched towards the dangerous dragon. "As a matter of fact, her goal right now is to return the souls of *your* leaders to the dragons. So before you go throwing insults around and snapping your teeth at people, you might want to find out about the person who's head you're about to bite off because she just might be the only person with the ability to save your kind!"

Sully seemed to calm down a bit. She looked around at all the people. It was quiet for a long time before she spoke again.

"I am sorry for my behavior. You must understand the pain we dragons went through those years ago. We lost trust in the gods and the humans. We now live in hiding. We cannot soar freely above the trees and mountains as we used to. Dragons are trapped although there are no physical chains that bind us." She looked at Jerriney.

"I can see now that this girl would not harm any being if it was her choice. Although she has the blood of a god, she is different than the normal demi-gods. You must also understand that those of mortal and immortal blood are usually born into this world to do the gods' fighting. I have never heard of one that does the opposite, but here she stands. I am honored to be in the presence of one that chooses a different, more peaceful path. Please, let us start over."

Sully straightened her neck so she loomed high

174

over the rest of them. Nicodemus motioned for Jerriney to come closer. The dragon looked at her.

"I am Sulanthreandius. Friends call me Sully. Who do I have the honor of meeting here?"

"I am Jerriney. Friends call me Jerri." She looked at Rhonwen. He smiled at her. "I bring with me Rhonwen, another Shifter, Drust, a blacksmith, and Muirnen, a traveler looking for a new home. We heard of you from the writings of a monk, and come to seek your aid."

† Chapter Seventeen †

When the dragon first appeared, Muirnen had stiffened and sunk deeper into his shroud. He hoped the dragon would not give any attention to him. Rhonwen noted his reaction to the dragon and was worried. Muirnen had seemed awfully quiet for the majority of their journey and Rhonwen was beginning to question whether or not he was really looking for a new home or if that was just a ruse. He needed to talk to him about this. Muirnen seemed like a potentially dangerous person though, so Rhonwen thought it would be best to try and expose him when everyone else was around. He decided to tell Jerriney of his decision as soon as they got a response from the dragon.

Jerriney had told Sully about their journey thus far, and that her goal now was to return the trapped souls of the High Dragons to their owners. Jerriney admitted that she did not have the slightest clue as to what they needed to do or who they needed to go to. This was why she was hoping Sully could help them. Maybe Sully could take the stones and this journey would be all over. Could it be that easy? She was getting home-sick so part of her wished that her journey had come to an end, but once she began to think about it, she felt a strange stirring inside, pulling her to continue the adventure. There was so much of her world she did not know about, so many things she could learn, and now that she knew she was part god, there was possibly another world she could explore.

"Where do the gods live anyway?" Jerriney thought to herself. *"Can I even get there?"* The dragons grating voice pervaded her thoughts.

"I have come to realize your mission is very important, not only to the dragons, but also to the whole of Amensdale. You may know that there are men after you, but the man in charge of them is more dangerous. You must be careful as you continue your journey. I am very grateful that you have brought these dragon souls to me. We have missed them dearly. You see, when the High Dragons began disappearing, we were in a great war with the gods and did not notice soon enough. We could not find who was stealing the souls of our leaders. In any normal circumstance, no one with ill intentions could get close enough to even see our leaders, as they knew the intentions of your heart the moment you made your decision. The gods

were a great distraction and since they had taken some of our magic away, our leaders were very vulnerable. They were not used to having to watch their back so carefully. Eventually all the High Dragons had disappeared and we had just begun to search for whoever was behind this evil doing. We found him. And we killed him. But we did not know what he had done with the souls. One very valiant mage was secretly working for us and knew that the evil man had used dark magic to enslave the souls in stones, but he did not know what he had done with the stones. Now we have five of them. I'm guessing that the man that is after you knows where the rest are. Your journey now, Jerriney, is to return the souls to their dragon owners. You must go to the High Dragons' resting place. I, unfortunately, do now know where that is. Nor do I know for sure who might know. But I know a dragon that is far older and wiser than I. He might know where the High Dragons' bones rest, or at least he might know someone who can tell you."

"Where is this dragon you speak of?" Jerriney asked Sully.

"*He takes refuge in the grottos to the west. Where the sea meets the mountains.*"

"Where the sea meets the mountains?" Drust

questioned the dragon. "There is no such place. It is not on any maps."

"It is not known to man. Man cannot fly and see how immense the land they live on truly is." Sully smiled at the bewildered group. *"Look at your map. The southernmost west area is blank. Man has not traveled there yet. That is where a small group of mountains are. That, is where the dragon you seek lives."*

"Does he have a name? Something he goes by that we can call him so he knows we are friends? I shall not like to have the same greeting you gave us, and I mean that in no offense," Rhonwen said to Sully.

"He has many names. He is the oldest of my kind that I know of. I should think that if you call him Bar'diin, he will know you mean no harm. He was given that name a long time ago, when man first came to this land. He helped the men of old run out the goblins so they gave him the name Bar'diin, which means goblin's bane. No one speaks that dialect anymore so he will surely listen once he hears that name."

"How will we get there? Dashlegar's men must be near upon us and if we head west they may likely cut us off if they are heading north or south," Drust pointed out.

"He makes a valid point. Plus, it would take us days to go by horse. We do not have many provisions and since the land is not settled yet, there are no villages to stop and replenish our packs, and we have no way of telling if we are going the right way because a lot of that territory has not been traveled before. I cannot see how we are to find Bar'diin without starving to death or getting lost," Jerriney added.

"The Hidden Door!" Nicodemus practically yelled.

"What is he talking about?" Rhonwen asked.

"Yes, of course. We couldn't use it before, but we can now." Melanthious walked toward the back of the dragon's cave. "Sully showed this to us when we first met her." He pointed to the floor around him where there were five triangles encircling him, points facing outward. If you were to connect all the triangles it would look like a star.

"What is it?" Rhonwen looked at one of the triangles. Its edges were jagged, as if carved from a blade not belonging to a human.

"A portal. It is like a magical doorway," Nicodemus told Rhonwen.

"It was carved long ago by the first dragons. There are many of them hidden, all over. Dragons made it for

the Shifters to travel from one place to the other more quickly. One Shifter stands in each triangle, those that wish to travel with them stand in the middle. The Shifters in the triangles then speak a certain incantation and they are taken to the place that is linked with the incantation. There is a special phrase for each spot." Sully touched the tip of her nose on one of the triangles.

"Why did the dragons do this for the Shifters? I know the dragons and our people have no quarrel, but I have never heard of one helping the other," Rhonwen asked Sully.

"Your people went through a situation similar to the dragons. The humans did not understand you so they cast you out. We were cast out by the humans too. We have a lot in common. Not only are we creatures of peace, but we have more power than humans could imagine, and we could easily take back what is rightfully ours but choose not to."

"Now that we have you amongst us, Rhonwen, we have a Shifter for each triangle. Nicodemus is old enough to know the incantation to take us northwest. We can leave anytime, and return the same way." Draxx turned to Rhonwen, waiting for his answer.

"I think it would be best if we left as soon as possible." Rhonwen looked at Jerriney. "Jerri, this is

181

your quest. When would you like to leave?"

"I agree with you. I've trusted your judgment ever since you were a cat. I still do." Jerriney stepped in the middle of the triangles. "Let's get on with this."

𝔇asbelgar was headed to a hidden hideout in the mountains, east of Rohalla Lake. He kept men there for when he needed an army. They were about to camp down for the night when Gulgor spotted something odd in the distance.

"Master, look!" He pointed to the east. There were raptors flying around something on the ground. "There's a bunch'a vultures over there. Some traveler must of had a bit 'o bad luck!" Gulgor chuckled at the demise of those who were now bird lunch. "Can we go have a look, Sir? See if they got anything shiny on them?"

"I suppose we might as well. Make sure the birds are putting good use to the traveler's meat." Dashlegar urged his horse forward, with Gulgor right on his heels.

As they came upon the dead travelers, the birds flew away, leaving a cloak of feathers to fall on the captain's men. Gulgor began rummaging through their pockets. The men's faces were barely discernible. The birds must have been there for quite a few hours. Dashlegar recognized his symbol on one of their over-shirts.

"Stop, Gulgor! These are my men from the mountains! They must have been ambushed." Dashlegar was angered, not that someone had killed his men, but because the men had allowed themselves to be killed.

"Whoever is in command of this group will pay! We will not stop tonight. We move on towards the mountains."

"Should we burn the remains, sir?" One of Dashlegar's men asked.

"No. They do not deserve such an honorable action. They failed their task. Let the wild animals feast on their flesh." Dashlegar continued on to find the man in charge of these dead men.

They reached their hideout that very night. Dashlegar found the man who was in charge of the men who had been killed.

"You there!" he yelled. "Why are my men dead out there being eaten by birds rather than doing their duty?" Dashelgar asked him not to kindly.

"Wu-what do you mean, sir?" The grey-haired male replied.

"The men you dispatched last week to scout are dead, supper for the birds of prey. How am I supposed to find the girl when your men cannot do their job?"

"I'm sorry sir, I did not know." The man wrung his hat in his hands. "As for the girl, I think I saw them but a day ago. Passing by, sir."

"What? You saw the white haired girl?" Dashlegar was enraged at the fact that he had not gone to investigate where she was going.

"Y-yes, sir."

"Then why are you not following her!! You should not be here now! I will have you killed for this. Where did she go, you insolent fool?" Dashlegar had him by the collar of his shirt now.

"Sh-she was with three other people. They headed s-south. Looked like they was lookin' to the mountains for something. I r-reckon they was goin' to the dragon you says lives there." The second the man finished his sentence, Dashlegar took his dagger and slit his throat.

"Someone clean this up!" He yelled as he walked to the exit of the cave.

𝔍erriney squinted as she stepped out of the dark cave. They had successfully transported southwest of

184

Sully's cave and had just found their way out of a twisting cavern.

"I don't see why they had to carve that one so far into the caves. And in a maze too!" Nicodemus complained as he exited the mouth of the cave into the sunlight.

"Can you tell if we are in the right location?" Drust asked.

"Of course we are! I remembered the correct incantation perfectly. There is no way I could have got it wrong," Nicodemus replied.

"We are by the ocean, so that should answer your question Drust," Draxx reassured him.

"How are we supposed to find the dragon Bar'diin now? We have no clue where he lives except in this general location," Drust continued, still worried they might be in the wrong place.

"There are markings here that signify a dragon lifting into flight. That should be a good enough clue as to where we should look," Jerriney said. Drust now felt embarrassed that he did not look at his surroundings before making assumptions that they were on the wrong track.

"Let us just walk along the shore for now. Cool off in the waters. I can't imagine you get to see the ocean very often, Jerriney, coming from Ascillia. Or even you Drust!" Rhonwen said. "The ocean is not like the lakes and ponds you are accustomed to."

They walked along the beach while they searched for more clues as to where the dragon might sleep. They eventually stopped and made a fire when the sun started to go down.

The group was eating their supper when Nazema, who had kept to herself for the majority of the time since they had come upon Jerriney, suddenly stood up and pointed to the ocean horizon.

"What is it Nazema?" Melanthious said as he looked towards where she was pointing.

The sun had not yet disappeared and made a glorious painting of reds and oranges on the water as it fell lower in the sky. There, in front of the sun, was a large shape just under the surface of the ocean, getting larger as it came closer to shore.

"It's a dragon!" Drust said excitedly.

They could all see the large figure clearly now and it was indeed, a dragon. Suddenly it leapt out of the water, droplets rained down from its wings as it gained altitude. It was heading right towards them, and quickly.

"He doesn't look very happy," said Rhonwen.

Muirnen reached for his sword.

"No!" Jerriney said. "Do not do anything that would make him think we are enemies!"

The great, white dragon soared above them and roared tremendously. He circled above them once and then landed a ways behind them. Jerriney and her friends quickly turned around to see what he was doing and saw him charging towards them, maw open ready to produce flame.

"Bar'diin!" Jerriney yelled as loud as she possibly could. Her small voice could not be heard above the dragon's grumblings, but everyone else, even the dragon, felt something in the air stir and suddenly push through their very beings as if a wave of air had assaulted them. The dragon suddenly stopped and closed his mouth. Smoke rolled out of his nostrils. He had a shocked expression on his face.

"Bar'diin," she said again. "We do not come to harm you."

The dragon stared for a while and then said, *"No one has called me that in centuries, little godling. How is it that you, a spawn of mine enemy, know one of my most treasurable names?"*

Jerriney swallowed her fears that had created a lump in her throat. "A dragon we call Sully gave it to us. She lives to the east, in the Promoka Mountains. She told us you could help us."

The dragon thought for a bit. *"And why do you think that I would help the very being that took away my powers and forced me to go into eternal hiding? What could I possibly gain from your egoistic dealings?"* The dragon stared intensely at Jerriney, anger clearly apparent in his eyes.

"Our quest will aid your kind, mighty dragon," Rhonwen tried to help.

"How so?"

"I have five of the lost High Dragons' souls that were trapped in stones. Sully told us that we needed to return them to their owners. She said you would know what to do," Jerriney bluntly said.

"I can certainly tell you are eager to be on with this task. I will not waste any precious time asking how you came to acquire such valuable a package. Your quest is indeed of the utmost importance. I am very surprised to hear this. My old ears have trouble believing what you have just said. Would you mind showing them to me?"

"Yes, of course." Jerriney stepped closer to the dragon and took out the blue stones. They shimmered brilliantly in the setting sun. She laid them on the ground before Bar'diin.

"There are six stones here." Bar'diin had a quizzical look on his face. *"You just told me you had five of the High Dragons' souls."*

"One I found separate from the others. It's a dragon's tear," Jerriney answered.

The white dragon dipped his nose low and touched the stones. As he slowly touched each one, they emitted a soft glow as if the souls inside knew he was kin.

"These truly are the missing High Dragons' souls!" he exclaimed. *"And you are right about this one."* He touched his snout to the stone that had moving silver tendrils. *"It is very rare that you should find a dragon tear rather than be given one personally."* He lifted his head up and allowed Jerriney to put the stones back in her pouch.

"I do not know the location of the High Dragons' bones; however, I know how you can find where they are at. There is a shrine to the east. It has been there for years. It was built when the humans valued our trust. The shrine was used to speak to the dragons when they were not around. If someone needed help or advice, they would make the trek to the shrine and convene with the dragons. It was also a way for those whose dragon had died, but had not yet been born into

189

another body, to speak to their departed friends. They
will know where it is."

"Thank you Bar'diin. I am glad we sought you out." Rhonwen bowed to the dragon. "I think we should go now."

"Before you leave, I must apologize for my greeting to you. I sensed the immortal blood in your two companions and was enraged that the gods dare step foot on my land. I am slightly put back by your behavior, Jerriney. Usually gods and their descendants are rude and do not care for the survival of other things. I am very glad you have acted not of your kin."

"Thank you, Bar'diin. That is very kind of you," Jerriney said to him. "I know I am half god, but you said you sensed that two of us were of immortal blood. I think you are mistaken, no offense towards you."

The dragon straightened his neck. *"No. My senses are quite right. The other one is there, the furthest from me. The one whose face is blocked by his hood."* Bar'diin stared at Muirnen.

"Muirnen?" Jerriney said confused. "You have immortal blood?"

Muirnen had gone stiff. His thoughts whirled around his head, trying to find a way out of this situation without harming his mother's plans. He decided it was best not to deny it. It was pointed out by a dragon, who was very wise so there was no way he could argue that he was fully human. He took his hood off.

"Yes. It is true," Muirnen simply stated.

"Why did you not tell us this?" Rhonwen questioned him. "I knew he wasn't worth trusting," he mumbled to himself.

"You did not ask. I did not think it was important for you to know whether I was human or not. I told you my business. You asked no more of me." Muirnen hoped he would still have their trust after this.

"I suppose he has a point," Jerriney said. "We did not query him about the nature of his blood," she said, turning from Rhonwen to Muirnen.

"This may not be the only thing we don't know about him." Rhonwen's voice reverberated through Jerriney's head. *"We should still keep an eye on him. He seemed taken aback by this."*

"Let us not dwell on this at this moment. We need to be going before Dashlegar gets wind of what we're trying to do." Rhonwen told the group. "I assume there is another Hidden Door near Koed since the dragons' shrine is near that town. Am I correct Nic?"

"Why yes! There is one hidden in a small forest

191

just north of Koed." The old shifter gladly shared his knowledge.

"I suggest you leave while it is dark. That forest you speak of hardly deserves to be called a forest. It is a very small collection of trees barely big enough to provide shelter for deer. You could be easily spotted and we still want to keep the secrecy of these portals so that mortals do not go snooping about and scrape additional lines into the triangles. Who knows what would happen then." Bar'diin turned around and headed for a cave nearby. Jerriney and the rest of the group returned to the cavern and wound their way through the maze-like tunnels back to where the Hidden Door was located. Rhonwen, Draxx, Nazema, Nicodemus, and Melanthious each stood on a triangle and Nicodemus began chanting the phrase that would take them to Koed.

"𝔚here did you send them?" Dashlegar calmly asked the shackled green dragon.

"They are days ahead of you by now. You would not be able to catch them," Sully snarled at Dashlegar.

"You, my little pet, are not in the position to tell me what I can and cannot do." Dashlegar was walking back and forth in front of the dragon as his men struggled to keep her down.

Nicodemus and the Shifters had left not too long ago. Sully had been feeling lonely and let her guard down when Dashlegar's men surprised her. She tried to fly away, but they had chains with big, heavy hooks on the end. They threw them at her wings and tore her membranes, not only making it impossible to fly if she got free, but they caught onto her wing joints and pulled her down. Once her wings were out of the way, she whipped her neck around, snapping at them, trying to get them to run away or at least knocked over. They eventually had chains around her maw and ankles and had dragged her into her cave. She was completely vulnerable now.

"Do whatever you want to me. I can last ages without giving in. I am not like you, puny human." An odd noise came from her throat and she pulled her head back.

"She's going to breathe fire!" One of the men said.

"Run away!" another said.

"Hold your chains men! If a single one of you runs away, I will kill all of you!" Dashlegar scolded his men. He looked back at Sully, and then got a face full of dragon spit.

193

"Ha! She spit on you!" the man holding one of her ankle chains said. They all laughed at the captain's slimy bath.

"Imbeciles! You'll all pay for this!" Dashlegar turned away from Sully and wiped some of her spit off his face. "Gulgor!"

"Yes, mi lord!" The goblin ran to him, trying not to laugh. He had been hiding behind a rock before the dragon spit because he was afraid of her.

"Give me something to wipe this off with."

Gulgor went back to the horses and grabbed one of the men's extra shirts.

"Here you are, mi lord." Gulgor handed him the shirt.

"Hey! That's my shirt!" Someone yelled. Dashlegar wiped the saliva off his face and threw the shirt back at its owner.

"Enough of this! It's time for you to die." Sully pulled her head back as far as the chains would allow her. This time you could tell she was getting fire ready. She opened her jaws and thrust her head towards Dashlegar. In an instant, the captain spun around, pulling out his sword as he did, and plunged it deep into the dragon's throat before the fires could escape.

He stood there, sword imbedded in her throat,

194

making sure she was dead. Once her eyes rolled into the back of her head he jerked the sword free. Sully's head dropped to the ground. Blood spilled out of her throat. The men dropped their chains.

"You just killed a dragon!" a short man said. "They're almost completely wiped out you know! Soon, none will be around. My kids won't ever get to see one!" He was outraged that this man could be so cold as to kill such a majestic beast.

"I'll kill you too if you don't leave immediately," Dashlegar replied, returning to his passive demeanor. The man quickly left the cave.

"Sir, you didn't get what we was lookin' for," Gulgor pointed out. Dashlegar was kneeling at Sully's head. He pulled out an extremely sharp dagger.

"There's still a way. And this time there's no way she can hold it from me." Dashlegar grinned and plunged the dagger into her eye socket.

✝ Chapter Eighteen ✝

Draxx suggested they camp the rest of the night on a hill outside the forest. They figured that if they were a ways from the Hidden Door, no one would expect anything suspicious and would just think they were travelers. Plus, they had a good view of the town and could see if anyone came in or out of Koed. Jerriney wanted to push on to the town and get supplies and continue to the shrine, but Rhonwen said that Dashlegar's men could be anywhere and they needed to rest so that they were at full strength. They still needed provisions though, so Drust went into town before the shops closed. He got there a little too late and the shops were already shut for the night, but he managed to get some dried beef the butcher was going to throw out. They would have to go back in the morning. When Drust returned they took turns keeping watch while the rest slept.

Muirnen was the third to be on watch. The rest of the group was in a deep sleep so he thought now would be a good time to speak with his mother. He grabbed his waterskin and headed away from the group, but facing Koed so that he could still keep watch. When he got far enough away that they couldn't hear him, he dug a small hole in the ground, about the size of a dinner plate. Muirnen then poured water into the hole. He waved his hand slowly over the water using his magic to seal the holes in the dirt so that the water would not soak in. Instantly the water rippled, his mother's face appearing.

"My love, what have you found out for me?" she said in a loving voice. Muirnen found this very odd as she had never acted this way.

"I do have something for you this time, not much though, but first," he paused for a couple seconds, "are you ill mother?"

"Ha! No, I am perfectly fine. I just have not heard from you in so long. I need to hear you have progress." A malicious smile replaced her loving countenance.

"Ah, well we met some new Shifters, four of them, and Jerriney was telling them of her journey before we ran into them. They were asking her questions, and she mentioned that she did not know who her parents were.

197

I can get no further information from her. She told me her aunt and uncle were on a long vacation, but she gave me no names." Muirnen looked to the town.

"I see. Well, thankfully, I have been doing some research of my own. I know the girl's surname, Criterious. I looked into that monk you mentioned. He too had the name of Criterious. I believe this Demeter has a sister. I think she is that retched girl's mother. I can finally have my revenge with this woman."

"What shall I do now? Should I come home?" Muirnen had begun to have feelings for this group of characters. He wasn't sure whether or not he wanted to return to the land of the gods.

"No! I'm not done with you yet. I am done with the girl though. Kill her." She grinned widely.

"What?" Muirnen's head snapped down to the image of his mother. "You want me to kill Jerriney? Why? She has no quarrel with you. She has done you no wrong." He was distraught with the thought of having to slay this unique female.

"Do as I say child!" She yelled at him, the water pulsing in response to her booming, ethereal voice. "She is the spawn of your father and a mortal! Our blood is tainted and it must be removed." Muirnen's mother looked sternly at him, anger billowing in her eyes.

With that, the illusion of her face disappeared from the water. Muirnen released his magic and allowed the water to seep into the ground. He looked to the town again, pondering on this impossible task he was assigned. The sun was just beginning to rise, and he noticed a group of men heading into the town. He used his godly powers to zoom in on the group. There was a man on a horse yelling at a goblin below him. Muirnen sensed that this was the man they were watching out for. He quickly returned to the rest of the sleeping members.

"Rhonwen!" Muirnen said as he shook him awake.

"What is it?" Rhonwen groggily said. He squinted in the morning light.

"A group of men just went into Koed. I believe it was Dashlegar and his followers. There was a goblin with him," Muirnen told him as the others began to wake.

"When?" Rhonwen was still a little asleep.

"Just now! What's our plan? We still need more supplies. Are we still going in?" Muirnen asked. Rhonwen could see concern on his face, and was puzzled. It was not like Muirnen to be so involved in what they were doing. Usually, he just followed, not speaking or asking questions.

"Well, um, I guess we have to discuss this. I didn't realize he would be so close. I thought he would be a couple days apart from us. Do you know if he is aware that we are here?" Rhonwen was finally waking up.

"No, I don't think he knows we're close to the town," Muirnen replied.

Jerriney and the others were awake now, looking through their packs to see if there was any kind of food they could have for breakfast.

"We need to go into town," Jerriney said. "We need food. We're completely out. We ate the rest of the bread last night with the dried meat."

"If you go in there Jerriney, he'll know. The town is too small to keep safely hidden," Drust said. "We need to hurry to the shrine."

"We can't last without food though! Last night's meal was not enough to get our strength up. If we happen to run into Dashlegar later, or something else that wishes to harm us, we won't last long," Jerriney added.

"I have an idea," Melanthious said.

There was a short pause as they waited for him to continue. When he didn't, Rhonwen prodded him on. "Go on."

"Nic, Drazz, Nazema, and I will go into town and get the supplies we need. We can also stall Dashlegar, if needed, and see how much he knows. He doesn't know we're with you. We can meet up at a later time, somewhere safer." Melanthious stood up.

"That sounds like a good idea. How will we know when and where to meet you?" Jerriney asked.

"We are Shifters, like Rhonwen. We are linked all the time, even when we did not know each other existed. He can hear our thoughts, and we his," Nicodemus explained.

"Alright, let's go then, and get a good distance away from this man." Rhonwen started packing up his things. The others did the same.

Once they had all their belongings gathered, they split up, the four Shifters headed toward Koed and Jerriney, Rhonwen, Drust, and Muirnen headed towards the Dragon Shrine. It would be nightfall before they reached the shrine.

When they got to town, Draxx and his fellow Shifters got the supplies they needed. Then, they scouted the town for Dashlegar and his men. They found them in a crowded bar.

"He reeks of Dark Magic," Draxx whispered to the rest of the Shifters. "Shield your mind, do not use magic except for communication between the four of us, and most certainly do not try and get into his mind. That would be the easiest and quickest way to find out if he knows where Jerriney is going, but we don't know if he has blocks on his mind as well. He could hurt us very easily, and brutally, with his Dark Magic." They nodded in response.

The four walked up to the counter and sat by the bar, close enough to Dashlegar that they could eavesdrop on him, but far enough away that he would not suspect them of anything.

"What can I get for you folks?" The bartender asked as he wiped out a mug with a dirty rag.

"Water and bread is fine," Melanthious responded. "We are just resting from a long day's travel."

The bartender left for a short while and came back with stale bread and plenty of water, then returned to cleaning with his dirty rag. The Shifters sat and nibbled on the bread while they tuned their extra sensitive hearing to the captain's group.

"What'll we do with the dragon's brain, sir?" the goblin asked Dashlegar.

"I'll send a man to the mage with it. He might like

to examine it further," Dashlegar replied as he pushed around the lump of grey stuff the cook called mashed potatoes.

"Where did you say we were going?" asked one of the men.

"Do any of you pay attention?" Dashlegar yelled. "The dragon told the girl that she needed to return the dragon souls to their original owners. That would be the bones of the High Dragons. We are going to stay here for the night and see if the girl comes this way. Then we will head to where the High Dragons' bones are and surprise them when they get there," he said while examining a green bean that had odd fuzzy brown spots.

"Do we 'ave to stay here? This food is 'orrible!" The goblin complained.

"If you wish to leave, then leave. I do not care what you do with your worthless life," Dashlegar remarked calmly as he pushed his plate aside.

Draxx stood up and looked at the others, hinting that it was time to go.

"So, where exactly is this shrine?" Jerriney asked anyone who knew.

"Well, Bar'diin didn't really go into detail where it was located. We should be near it though. I can sense it," Rhonwen responded.

"I wonder how big it is." Drust speculated whether it was monumental, or just some small statue. He soon got his answer.

He was looking at his feet, watching the dust puff up and whirl around, when he walked right into the Dragons' Shrine. It wasn't humongous, but it was no small thing either. The stone shrine was twice as tall as Drust, and he was the tallest in their group of four, and wide enough to take two to wrap their arms around it. On the shrine were carvings of dragons, flying around the obelisk, coiling all around it up to the very top. Plants had sprouted at the base and were climbing up, as if on a tree.

"It's amazing!" Jerriney gasped. She had never seen anything like this in Ascillia or anywhere else for that matter.

"It most certainly is." Drust agreed as he rubbed his head where he had hit the stone.

"We must not waste any time. It is a beautiful thing, but we are on an important mission," Rhonwen said.

"Right," Jerriney said. She took the pouch from her

side and then paused. "I do not know what I'm supposed to do. I know we came here to communicate with the dragons, but how do we do that? Do I need to do something with the stones?"

"I don't think we need the stones. Bar'diin said anyone could come here if they wanted to speak to a dragon," Muirnen reminded them.

"But how?" Jerriney asked again. She walked up and gently touched one of the dragons on the shrine. She felt a pull on her mind. She jerked her hand off the stone and backed away. They all looked at the dragon she had touched; light was coming out of the lines that formed it. Then, all of the dragons had light coming out of them. They seemed to start moving up the shrine.

"What's happening?" Jerriney asked.

"Well I don't know!" Rhonwen retorted.

The dragons moved faster and faster until they couldn't make out any forms and the Dragons' Shrine seemed to be covered in light. It became brighter and brighter, and a faint whirling noise could be heard until it suddenly stopped and all was quiet—nothing moved. The dragons that had been carved on the shrine were no longer there.

Just as quickly as it stopped, the noise began again. They saw all the dragons that were previously on the shrine fly out the pointed tip where they split into five groups and came down towards Jerriney and her friends, and merge back together, forming a glorious dragon. It shimmered prismatic in the moonlight, and they could see through it, like a ghost. Jerriney thought it looked vaguely familiar.

"Hello, Jerriney," the illusion said with the voices of all the dragons that had ever existed echoing through the night.

"You know me?" Jerriney walked toward the glistening dragon. "You do seem familiar, but I'm not sure."

"We met recently," the dragon said, "but not all of us." It smiled.

"Sully?" Jerriney queried.

"Yes, but you are currently speaking to all the dragons of the past. We decided to choose my form because you were familiar with it. That is also the same reason my voice is heard most over the rest."

"But you are not dead. We just saw you a couple days ago," Rhonwen said.

"That is true, but my body was slain. After you left, I was full of loneliness. I had become so accustomed to having the Shifters around that I was filled with grief when they left. That is when Dashlegar's men caught me by surprise. I tried to flee, but they managed to shackle me. I will not go further into details. In the end, Dashlegar killed me, and then that horrid man took his tainted knife and cut my brain out. From it, he learned where I sent you by using Dark Magic." The form looked solemn.

"For this reason, we must not tally with conversation. I know you have many questions, not only for me, but for the other dragons as well, but you must continue your journey. Since I have joined my kin, I know everything they do; therefore, I know where the High Dragons' bones rest. South of here there is a mountain range that melds into a forest that is hiding a village and its citadel, along with a lake. To get to the resting place of the High Dragons you must first go south of here and then begin heading west. First, you will come upon the Lonely Lake. Follow its northern bank and you will see Sudonia Citadel. Avoid this place at all costs. Leave the water line and continue west. You will eventually come upon the village of Sudar. The people here are plagued by the man in the citadel so you will be safer here, but be watchful. From Sudar, go north into the mountains. There you will find where the High Dragons' bones lay." The dragon paused and looked at the horizon.

"We must leave now, before the sun comes up. Please, Jerriney, hurry. What you are about to do will change the course of history for dragons and humans, and all the rest of Amensdale. Should you fail, this land will fall into turmoil and dragons will cease to exist. Remember what we have told you." Sully and the other dragons' voices faded into the night. Then all the dragons burst into the sky and returned to the shrine and all was silent.

𝕿𝖍𝖊𝖞 met up with the Shifters southwest of the shrine. They had already made camp and had food ready to eat. Jerriney, Rhonwen, Drust, and Muirnen ate while the Shifters told them what had occurred.

"I think they killed my Sully!" Nicodemous yelled distraughtly. Jerriney looked at Rhonwen.

"They did, or rather, Dashlegar did," Rhonwen told him, "but do not be saddened, you can still see her and speak with her. She is the one we saw at the shrine. Whenever you like, you can go visit her." He tried reassuring him.

Nicodemus looked down, suddenly lost in his thoughts.

"Dashlegar knows what we are trying to do, but I

don't think he is aware of our location. I suggest we move forward as quickly and as soon as possible," Draxx suggested.

"Yes, Sully told us that we need to go south, where it is unmarked on the map," Muirnen suddenly piped in.

"We will get some rest and head out as soon as we can." Rhonwen wanted to make sure Jerriney got some sleep even though the sun was already rising. They finished their food and settled down, still keeping guard.

𝕽honwen woke Jerriney around midday. The others had already packed up most of the camp. Rhonwen did not want to wake Jerriney until the last moment so that she would be well rested and have plenty of strength.

Once Jerriney had eaten, they headed west. They could see a forest ahead, and decided to walk along its edge until they reached the lake that the dragons at the shrine had mentioned. Jerriney thought that the lake would be a nice place to stop and wash up a bit.

They had reached the edge of the forest and were talking about how their journey was almost at an end when they suddenly heard rustling in the bushes. Everyone stopped and glanced into the forest. Just when they were about to continue on their way they heard someone yell "Now!" A group of men jumped out of the trees and from behind bushes.

"Kill everyone but the girl!" a man yelled. Jerriney and the others unsheathed their weapons and looked for who was giving orders while they defended themselves.

"It's Dashlegar!" Draxx yelled.

"How did he get ahead of us?" Rhonwen yelled back as he parried a blow from a crooked nosed man. "We kept watch all night!"

"I don't know!" Draxx replied as he was nearly pummeled by a large brute running at him.

While his men were fighting, Dashlegar was watching. He was sure this would be the end of the silver haired girl and her annoying friends.

"I saw your little camp this morning as I was leaving Koed. I used Dark Magic to see if it was really you. Of course you were all talking to each other so no one was keeping watch. While you were distracted I hurried my men into the forest to wait for you. I was surprised that you were ahead of me. I figured you'd still be with that old dragon." Dashlegar said as he stepped out of the forest. "Once I realized you would probably be headed to the High Dragons' bones, I decided I would just ambush you before you even knew where the tomb was. Oh! And you are right by my destination so I won't have to travel far. I thank you." He grinned maliciously at them and bowed, mocking them.

"You won't get what you're looking for, Dashlegar. I won't let you have it." Jerriney challenged him.

"I'll just have to take it from you then. Shouldn't be too hard. You're just a child," he said as he walked toward Jerriney.

"Jerriney, be careful! He uses Dark Magic. It is much stronger than what you wield!" Rhonwen yelled at her as he plunged his broadsword through one of Dashlegar's men.

"Ha! I do not think I will *need* to use magic." Dashlegar laughed. He looked at Jerriney and unsheathed his rapier.

Jerriney readied her sword. She tried to remember everything that Ron had taught her as she prepared for him to attack.

$\mathfrak{G}$ulgor had made sure he was behind Dashlegar and the rest of the men when they hid in the forest. He really did not like all this chasing and killing of people. All he wanted was some company and maybe a couple shiny things. He actually kind of liked the silver haired girl; the sun made her hair shiny. He liked that. When Master yelled for everyone to attack the Shiny Haired Girl and her friends, he stayed hidden behind the trees. Master didn't care that Gulgor didn't listen to him. Come to think of it, Master didn't care about Gulgor at all. He even said he didn't care if Gulgor left him. Master never showed appreciation to Gulgor, even for all the nice things Gulgor did for Master.

Now what's master shouting at? Oh, it's the pretty Silver Haired Girl. Her hair is so shiny when it moves in the sunlight. Gulgor would like to have some of that hair. Maybe make a necklace. Then Gulgor can see pretty, shiny hair whenever he wants. Shiny Haired Girl treats her friends nicely. Gulgor should like to see how it feels to be treated nicely. Maybe Gulgor should leave Master. But that would be mean. But Master is always mean to Gulgor, why not Gulgor be mean this time? Yes, Gulgor leave. Take Master's bag of shiny things he told Gulgor to watch. Gulgor go find people who treat him like Shiny Haired Girl treats her friends.

212

The goblin took a final look at the girl with silver hair, then he grabbed Dashlegar's loot bag, turned around and left the forest. He decided he would try and find people like him, other goblins. He thought it would be best if he went back to his homeland. He didn't remember it much because Dashlegar had taken him from it when he was a young gobbling. He was going to head back to Koder Docks. Gulgor finally felt like he was doing something he wanted, and not what that mean, arrogant man told him to do. Gulgor was finally happy.

𝔍erriney had been fighting off Dashlegar while her friends took care of his men. She thought she saw at least a dozen of them jump out of the forest so she knew she would not have help for a while. Jerriney was starting to become afraid that this was the end. Her strength was failing and Dashlegar hadn't seemed to even break a sweat yet. She wondered why he didn't use his magic and just get it over with. She thought about trying to find her innate magic and use it, but she was afraid that would provoke him to retaliate with his own.

She was just about to see if there was a way she

213

could use her magic to help strengthen her when her foot suddenly hit a rock. Dashelgar lunged at her. Jerriney blocked his attack, but lost her balance and fell to the ground. She let go of her sword so she could use her hands to break her fall. Dashlegar stood over her, blade tip at her throat.

"Looks like I win." He smiled at her.

"No you don't," Jerriney heard Muirnen say as he ran up from the side and tackled Dashlegar to the ground. Dashlegar quickly took advantage of the situation and hit Muirnen on the head with the pummel of his sword.

"Annoying little twit!" he exclaimed as he stood up and straightened his shirt.

While he was distracted, Jerriney was able to stand up and look inside herself for the magic she knew she had. Dashlegar saw her concentrating deeply with her head down and her eyes closed. He laughed at her.

"You think you can defeat me with magic, child? You have hardly even touched your powers and you think you can harm me?" He started walking towards her, leaving his weapon behind.

Jerriney opened her eyes and jerked her head up.

"I'm not a child," she said through clenched teeth.

Jerriney yelled to the heavens as she unleashed all

her stored up power, her hair and clothing flailing in all directions. Dashlegar was violently pushed through the air by an unseen force and was smashed against a tree.

Dashlegar fell limp to the ground. He ached all over. He coughed. Blood. He couldn't believe this! This girl who had never consciously used magic in her life had almost broken his entire body! He was sure *something* was broke, possibly multiple bones. He looked up. All his men were dead. Jerriney stood looking at him, blood ran down from her nose. Her friends were now backing her up. He had lost this fight. He needed to get out. He looked at his fallen comrades again. *"I can use their souls."*

Dashlegar got to his knees. He stared intently at Jerriney, and then he closed his eyes.

"Stay back, Jerriney. We do not know what he is doing. I feel something stirring. If he uses Dark Magic you will want to be near the rest of us magic wielders," Nicodemus warned her.

"This isn't over." Dashlegar suddenly growled before he flung his arms out and screamed with his head tilted back. They saw black masses come out of the fallen men and rush toward him. They started circling Dashlegar so quickly it looked like a whirl-wind had started around him.

"What's happening?" Jerriney worriedly asked.

"He's turning his own men's souls into Dark Magic to transport him!" Draxx exclaimed.

"Shouldn't we stop him?" Drust asked.

"No! Dark Magic is very unpredictable! There's no telling what would happen if we touched him," Nicodemus replied.

They all watched as the black souls went faster and faster around Dashlegar, until they couldn't see him. Then, all of the sudden, it seemed as though the whirling forms exploded, tendrils of black light flying everywhere. Dashlegar was gone.

Jerriney stared open mouthed at the spot that, just seconds ago, Dashlegar occupied.

"How could he do that? Just use souls to take him elsewhere?" She looked at the Shifters.

"Dark Magic," Melanthious said. "He didn't use the souls themselves, but transformed them into magic he could use to his own will. He basically just killed those men a second time. Their souls no longer exist."

"That's horrible!" Drust said. "How can anyone do something like that? Even someone like Dashlegar?"

"Once you use Dark Magic it starts to change you. You could be a mage with the purest of hearts who just wants to study this magic to try and find how it becomes so powerful, and it will corrupt you. You do not notice it happen, but it takes a hold of you and uses you for its own bidding, which is always purely evil," Nicodemus told Drust.

"We need to move on. I'm sure he went to warn whoever he reports to of our being here." Rhonwen pointed out. "We can talk about your magic later," he added privately to Jerriney.

They started walking towards the lake. They were passing a boulder on the edge of the water when they heard a voice.

"E-excuse me."

They spun around and reached for their swords.

"No, no, no! I, I'm not one of Dashlegar's men!" A scrawny, middle-aged man said.

"Who are you then? And why are you hiding behind this rock?" Rhonwen asked, hand still on the hilt of his sword.

"My name is Fisher," the man said, fear seeming to vanish as he proudly stated his name. "I am the fisherman for the village Sudar, which is not far from here. I was minding my own business, doing my daily rounds checking the underwater cages, when I heard yelling and sword clashing. I peeked beyond this here rock to see what the ruckus was and noticed it was

217

Dashlegar's men and some strangers I did not know. I decided to stay and see the outcome of the battle. One, because I was scared chicken that if Dashlegar saw me running away he would kill me, and two, because I thought if you strangers did win, you might need some help since I'm sure you are completely unaware of the land to the west of us."

Rhonwen and the rest had relaxed as Fisher told them his story. He seemed as though he was going to tell them a lengthy tale so when he stopped they were still expecting him to continue. After a moment of silence that seemed like minutes long, Fisher hinted that it was their turn to speak.

"The end," he politely said.

"Yes, uh, well I guess we are in need of help. What is that black tower looming over there?" Rhonwen asked as he pointed north.

"That would be Sudonia Citadel. Home to, well we don't know his name. We just call him Dark Man. He has been there as long as we can remember and he has had our little town in fear for ages. We do whatever he says, no questions. Dark Man also has many men who frequently come into the village to collect from us virtually everything we have grown, caught, made, or are proud of, to take to Dark Man. If we are good he takes a little less. If we step just so slightly out of line, he leaves us with nothing. I would stay away from there if I were you. I hear he is a mage of the Dark Magic."

"Hm. Well right now we need rest and sustenance. You told us he takes everything from you, I'm guessing food as well, so I understand if you don't wish to share with us, but I assure you, any help you give us we will repay you and more," Rhonwen said.

"Quite the contrary actually. I will gladly give you a warm bed to stay in and plenty food. We don't have much, but we treat our guests like royalty. Although, we haven't had any guests in ages, but yes! Do follow me," Fisher said as he gestured for them to walk with him. "I also know that Dark Man will probably be on the lookout for you since I'm sure Dashlegar went to warn him. I can also provide hiding places where even Dashlegar himself could not find. We have been waiting forever for someone to come help us!" He continued on, grinning immensely.

"Isn't it odd that he is a fisherman and his name is Fisher?" Jerriney mentioned to Rhonwen.

"Actually, it's not. Long before you were born, everyone was called by their skill. For example, a blacksmith was called Smith or Smithy. One who baked bread was called Baker, a sheep herder Shepherd.

Eventually humans began to create the names you see today and they have a second name that was their skill. The people in this village must be so cut off from the rest of the world that they have not caught on to that tradition," Rhonwen informed Jerriney.

They walked along with Fisher as he told them more about Sudar. It took them a while to get to the town because he had to finish his rounds with the fish lines. They got there just as the veil of night was falling on the village. Fisher took them to an inn that his brother owned and they were greeted like they had slain the Dark Man the villagers feared so much. After they met the people at the inn they sat down to wait at a large table in what must have been the village's gathering room. Fisher told them that the whole village was bringing something from their home to share with them. They watched as the food poured in. Each person didn't have a lot, but they all brought more than they could probably afford. They feasted that night.

"Sire! Dashlegar has transported here and he is very wounded! He asks that you see him immediately!" A servant stormed into the mage's bedroom.

"Take me to him," the old mage grumbled. He was

way past his death date, but the Dark Magic he used kept him looking healthy and virtually impossible to kill by disease or other non-man made material. In order to do this, he had to go to his orb every day and allow the dark forces to enter him. The orb was his portal to Dark Magic. This was a very dangerous thing to do as demons and other unearthly things could come out, but by keeping the portal in the glass orb this kept the portal sealed, but still available, until he chose to use it again.

"Here we are." The servant opened the door to the citadel's infirmary.

"Go to the village and tell the women they must send their finest medics. If they do not, they will not get to keep their bread supplies tomorrow," the mage replied.

"Right away sire." The mage had never told anyone his name so he was usually called sire.

"What happened, Dashlegar? Last I heard, you were coming to check in with me and now you appear in my house fighting death."

"I saw the girl heading this way so I ambushed her. I didn't think she was capable of using her magic." Dashlegar attempted to tell the mage what had occurred, wheezing the whole time. His ribs were cracked so he was having troubles breathing. "Slammed me hard," he paused to cough, "against a tree."

"She will probably be in town by now, I suppose. I'll send a quill and some parchment down to you. Write down the description of the girl and her friends. I will give it to the men doing routes so they can look for her. You better hope she doesn't succeed in returning those souls or you will pay for your foolishness. You could have easily defeated her had you used your magic from the start!" The mage stormed out of the room, his cloak billowing about him as he returned to his bedroom.

† Chapter Nineteen †

"**So** you know where the High Dragons' bones are?" Jerriney asked Fisher.

"Yes, of course! Their tomb is our only hope. People of the village go there frequently to pray to the dragons and ask for forgiveness for the sins of our forefathers. If dragons were still around, I'm sure the village of Sudar would not be so poor and the Dark Man would be vanquished by now," Fisher replied.

They had spent the night at the inn that Fisher's brother owned. It was not used very often, but it had been cleaned up quite nicely for Jerriney and her fellow travelers. They had to get up at the first sight of light breaking over the horizon so they could hide from the Dark Man's men who came early every morning to collect Morning Dues. They also came after lunch and right before supper.

After the Dark Man's men had left that morning, Fisher made a nice hot breakfast for Jerriney and her friends and she told him why they had come. She didn't think that they needed to hold anything back from these people. They seemed so eager to help them without even knowing why they had come. Fisher was elated that they were trying to return the High Dragons' souls. He thought they would soon be free from the evil mage's terror.

"Why don't the people of this village just leave if the mage takes everything from them?" Drust asked Fisher.

"It's not that easy. We would love to leave, and we have tried. He doesn't let us leave and the only way out is the way you came in. We are surrounded by mountains. We've looked for ways to go through them, but we always come out unsuccessful. The Dark Man has dropped his watch lately though, making it possible that a couple people could slip by, but all of us are too weak to make it very far as a whole group. We wouldn't last long outside of this town," Fisher explained. "That is why no one here will rat you out to the guards. Everyone thinks you will save us."

There was a brief moment of silence. Before anyone could say anything Fisher continued. He did not want them to have the chance to say that they did not come to save the village.

"If you are all done with breakfast, we should be heading for the tomb," he said as he picked up the empty plates.

"Yes, let us get started. I am eager to see what happens when we reunite the dragons' souls with the bones," Nicodemus said as he stood up.

They went and packed their belongings in case they would have to come back in a hurry and leave, and also to grab a couple things. They were walking to the tomb so Fisher told them to bring water and anything else that they might need.

They left shortly after breakfast was cleaned up. Rhonwen came up to Jerriney as they were leaving the village.

"I went for a walk earlier this morning to think for a bit. I noticed some flowers up ahead near the edge of the village. I want you to pick one. Make sure it has plenty petals on it."

Jerriney thought this was an odd request. "Why do you want me to pick a flower?"

"While we are walking, I want you to focus on finding your magic. You found it yesterday, but it took you a while to do it and you released it with little control. In a magical battle, you need to be able to summon your powers quickly and you will need to be able to control the outcome one-hundred percent of the time. It will be very dangerous if you do not master control over it. I have a feeling you will need to call upon your magic soon, so this is very important. Do you understand?"

"Yes, but what does a flower have to do with it?" Jerriney was still very confused.

"I want you to pluck the petals off with pure magic. No help from your hands and it has to be gentle and controlled. Find your magic, pull one petal off, release the magic, and repeat. I want you to work on quickly finding your magic. The more you practice, the sooner you will be able to do it without thinking. Once the petals on the flower are gone, find something on the ground, a rock, a twig, a blade of grass, and try to bring it to you, gently and slowly. If there is a bush or tree, pull a leaf off. Remember to release your hold on the magic after every time you succeed in your goal. I'm hoping this will help in the near future," Rhonwen told her as they came upon the flowers he had seen earlier. Jerriney picked a bright orange marigold.

"Is this enough petals?" she asked Rhonwen.

He smiled, "Yes that should do."

Jerriney did her best to concentrate on the lesson. She had never consciously summoned her magic until just yesterday, but she was persistent. Her first attempt brought only a slight movement of one of the petals. It had taken her a while to get any results at all so, when she saw the petal she was staring at move, she jumped in shock and dropped the marigold. Embarrassed, she looked at the others in front of her to see if they had noticed what had happened. They were still walking forward, talking amongst themselves so she swooped up the flower and hurried to catch up.

After seeing proof that she could purposely use her magic to move something, Jerriney began her concentration on the flower with a renewed confidence. It was not long before she could pluck a petal off and toss it to her side using only magic. At first, the movements were a little shaky, but as she continued plucking, it looked as if the petals jumped off the flowers, falling to the left and right of Jerriney and leaving a little trail.

Once the marigold's petals were gone, she focused on things around her. Soon, she was able to guide rocks to her hand or pull leaves carelessly off trees.

Before she knew it, they were at the tomb. It didn't look like much from the outside, just a hole in the mountains. Around the opening, the villagers had placed stone ornaments and flowers on the ground.

"Here we are," Fisher said. "It looks small from out here, but inside it's quite vast."

227

"Thank you, Fisher. I don't know how long this will take us. You can go back to the village so the guards don't miss you. We wouldn't want you getting in trouble because of us," Rhonwen told him.

"Yes, of course." He turned around to go back to the village and Jerriney started going in the tomb.

"Oh, uh, be careful, please," Fisher suddenly said as he spun around. "This tomb is the only hope my people have. I don't know what would happen to them if anything bad should happen to the High Dragons' bones."

"We will be respectful, I promise," Jerriney assured the man.

"Thank you." He nodded and then continued home.

Jerriney led her friends into the tomb. It was awkward at first. They had to walk single file and crouch with their backs against the ceiling, then they stumbled into an enormous room.

"Fisher wasn't kidding when he said vast," Drust said.

Inside the tomb, the complete skeletons of twelve High Dragons were laid out in a circle, their noses pointing in. Jerriney walked into the middle and looked around.

"Why are they all here like this?" she asked.

"When the mage cast the spell to trap the High Dragons in the stones, he made sure he had every single bone of the twelve dragons. He cast a spell on them as well," Nicodemus told them. "They cannot be removed from this tomb and there is no way for the souls to get in if they ever found a way to escape from those stones." He smiled at Jerriney. "I'm guessing the spell required them to be arranged in a circular fashion."

"How did the mage get them in here? Their heads alone are three times the size of a horse and we barely fit in the entrance!" Drust wondered aloud as he walked to one of the skulls.

"Again, he probably used a spell. There are many spells to move earth. He could have closed it after all the bones were in. There are also spells that can make objects smaller than they really are, although spells as such are very risky. The object might not be exactly how they were after you change them back to original size. I don't think he would have risked that," Draxx said.

"Do you know what to do with the souls now?" Rhonwen asked Jerriney.

"No. I haven't a clue. The scroll at the Abbey that Ron and I found didn't say anything about this part. It didn't even tell us where the bones were. The dragons at the shrine didn't say anything either."

Jerriney took the stones out. *"I'll just set them here. Maybe I don't really need to do anything,"* she thought to herself. She placed the stones on the ground in the middle of the dragon circle and stepped back.

"Nothing." Jerriney sighed. She turned around.

"Well, we brought them here. Nothing's happening. Do we leave now?" Drust said as he looked at Rhonwen and the rest of the Shifters.

Rhonwen shook his head. "I don't—"

"Hold on! Look!" Muirnen said, pointing to the stones. They all turned their attention to the middle of the room.

The five stones were glowing. They started to shake and lift off the ground. They hovered in the air for a while then whizzed off towards the dragon bones, each stone going toward a particular set. Once the souls got to the High Dragons they belonged to, the stones abruptly stopped. Jerriney stepped back in the middle of the circle. She felt like she was supposed to be there while this happened. The stones continued glowing brighter and brighter until the stone that encased each soul burst into dust. The souls flew up towards the ceiling and doubled back down and entered the skulls they once knew.

Jerriney was slowly turning in a circle, trying to watch all five souls. The gigantic skeletons started shaking. Jerriney stopped turning and decided to watch just one. They all seemed to be doing the same thing. As the bones shook, they moved into their corresponding sockets and then froze. The skeletons began to move. They got up on their feet and stretched their necks and wings, then each skeleton folded back their wings and looked at Jerriney. In their eye sockets were small blue flames.

"Jerriney." A voice formed out of nowhere and was heard throughout the room. It sounded strong, yet weak at the same time.

"Yes? Wha-what do you need?" Jerriney asked, slightly afraid.

"We thank you for returning our souls to the five of us. We are not free yet, though. You must go to the citadel a retrieve the seven of us that are missing. We cannot leave without them."

"Yes, I-I can do that. Could you help me in any way? Give me advice, or perhaps a magic spell that will help against the mage? Does he have a weakness?" Jerriney dearly hoped they could help her.

"No, we cannot help you. There is no time for questions. We will not last long like this and the mage

231

could come and seal us up again. He comes in every so often to check on our bones. You must go now, take no longer than a night's rest. Do this, and dragons will once again be able to thrive in Amensdale and our trust in humans will gradually return."

"But I need help! I've hardly had any experience with my magic and he is an expert in Dark Magic! You can't expect me to defeat him alone!" She pleaded with the High Dragons.

"Go now!" The voice boomed.

It shook the tomb and small rocks fell from the ceiling. The skeletons fell back into the place they had been when the group had walked in.

Jerriney picked up the dragon tear that she had placed in the middle of the circle with the rest of the stones. She defiantly walked back towards the exit, tears streaking down her face.

"You are not alone, Jerriney. All of us will help you get the rest of the souls," Drust told her.

"I don't want any of you to get hurt. This is my burden to bear. I will see it through myself," Jerriney said harshly. She was angry at the High Dragons. She had thought they would be of more help since they were the most revered dragons in the land.

Rhonwen pulled Drust back. "We'll discuss it

when we get back to the village, after we've rested and had a bit to eat. And after she's calmed down," he told him.

𝕿𝖍𝖊𝖞 returned to the inn just in time to eat supper. Fisher informed them that they had just missed the guards so they would not need to hide until the morning. The guards were asking about Jerriney, but no one said anything. Fisher had gone home after they finished eating. They were sitting around the fireplace when Rhonwen decided it was time to make a plan of action.

"I think it would be best if we fought this mage together. We will be stronger together," Rhonwen suggested.

"I appreciate your help, but I just feel like this is something I need to do alone. I don't want you guys getting hurt. You all have something to live for. I have no family left and there is only one person back home that will miss me." Tears formed in Jerriney's eyes, but she shook her head to dismiss her sadness, replacing it with determination. "I go alone."

"We don't want you getting hurt either, Jerriney. You have hardly tapped into your powers. At least let

233

us Shifters go with you," Draxx tried.

"No. I'm sure they will be on the lookout for us and I bet there are more eyes up in the citadel searching. It would be easier for just one to get in and stay hidden," Jerriney argued.

"She does have a point," Nicodemus stated.

"No!" Rhonwen blurt out while he quickly stood, knocking over his chair. "Jerriney, you are still a child, whether you accept that or not. You cannot go in there alone, I will not allow it." He pounded his fist against the table in frustration. Rhonwen calmed himself and looked sadly at Jerriney.

"You say you do not have anything to live for, Jerriney, but you do. You have barely just stepped into this world. There is so much you can do, and you do not need a family, you have all of us." Rhonwen gathered his emotions, picked up the chair, and sat back down.

"We can make a plan where we can still be stealthy. We'll go in small groups and meet up in a designated place. All we need is someone who knows the layout of the citadel. Drust, could you go get Fisher? I'm sure he knows someone who is forced to work there." Rhonwen was bent on making sure Jerriney did not go in without someone to back her up.

"The High Dragons said we only have a night to

234

rest. This plan you're trying to make could take days to come up with!" Jerriney said as she stood up.

"Jerriney, I have made the decision. You are not going alone," Rhonwen said without looking at her.

Jerriney looked at Nicodemus. He seemed to be the only one on her side. She hoped he might say something, but he seemed in a world of his own. She returned to her room. Somehow she would find a way in without the others.

✝ Chapter Twenty ✝

Muirnen was in his room laying on his bed and thinking to himself. He was still conflicted by his mother's order to kill Jerriney. *"I could do it while she's sleeping. Sneak into her room, take care of it, and leave before anyone knows. Then I wouldn't have to face them."*

Muirnen had become fond of this group of individuals. He didn't want to see them if he went through with this. He also didn't want to jeopardize Jerriney's mission. *"But someone else could finish it."*

"I hope you're not thinking of doing something stupid." Rhonwen's voice interrupted his thoughts. He was leaning on Muirnen's doorframe.

"No. What do you mean?" Muirnen sat up.

"You've been quieter than normal. Something seems to be bothering you," Rhonwen said as he stepped forward.

"I'm fine. Thanks for your concern," Muirnen said as he looked to the floor.

"I've been watching you Muirnen. I'm still

watching you. If you make a single move to harm Jerriney I will not hesitate to remove you from the face of the Earth," Rhonwen threatened him.

Muirnen did not take his eyes off the floor. Once Rhonwen saw that Muirnen was not going to respond, he left and returned to his room. Rhonwen did not like to be so harsh, but he thought it was necessary. He just wanted to make sure Jerriney was not in danger while they were supposed to be in a safe area. Rhonwen slept lightly that night.

𝕵erriney woke an hour before they had planned to get up. She had gone to sleep with her battle clothes on and had hidden her sword outside so she wouldn't have to make noise as she left. She went out of the inn and headed towards Fisher's house. She knocked on the door quietly.

"Fisher?"

Nothing. She knocked again, a little louder.

"Fisher?" She tried again.

He answered the door this time.

"What is it Jerriney? We're not supposed to wake for another hour."

"I know, but we're not doing it Rhonwen's way.

You're either going to help me get in that citadel alone or I'm finding a way in without your help," she said firmly.

He thought for a moment. "Well I don't want you going in blindly. One of you was going to be led in by a cook. I'll go and wake her and explain what's going on. We'll meet by the east wall. There's a door that's not guarded. Find it."

Jerriney went to find the door Fisher told her about while he went and got the cook that would lead her in. It wasn't that easy to find. It was still dark, and the citadel wall cast a shadow on her, making it even darker. She ended up having to retrace her steps when she thought she had gone too far. This time she walked with a hand against the stone wall so that she could feel the difference instead of relying on her eyes. It didn't take long before she felt stone change to wood. Jerriney stopped walking and looked at the door. She took a step back. The color of the door in the shadows was almost indiscernible from the stones. No wonder she had missed it the first time! While she waited for Fisher to show up she braided her hair. She used to always braid her hair before sparring with Ron. She had been missing him a lot lately. As she wound her hair back and forth, she felt he was with her, cheering her on.

It didn't take long before Fisher arrived with a portly woman. They went through the door, which opened into a store room.

"There is a tunnel that goes to the kitchen. We can go through there so the guards do not see you," the woman said.

"I will return to the inn and make sure your friends know what's going on when they wake up," Fisher told Jerriney.

He turned to leave. Jerriney quickly grabbed his arm to stop him.

"Something wrong, Jerriney?" Fisher asked, concern crossing his face.

"I just—" She stopped mid-sentence and bit her bottom lip. "I want to fight the mage alone, but this is my first time controlling my magic and when I'm done with that fight ..." She trailed off, unsure what would happen in the moments to come. "I might be too tired to fight anymore and there's sure to be many guards." Jerriney looked at Fisher.

"Don't worry. Your friends will come whether or not I tell them that you would like them too. Be strong, you'll do just fine." He smiled and left her with the cook.

Jerriney turned to the women, building up her

confidence for the fight ahead. The cook grabbed her hand and hurried her in the store room and to the trap door that led to the tunnel.

"This will go all the way to the kitchen. Once inside, I will show you a small hallway that goes to the stairs that leads to the mage's bedroom. The hallway was used for servant boys to take food to places in the citadel without running into other people and risking dropping the food. It goes to several different rooms, so there will be turns, but you need to just go straight, no turns at all, understand?"

"Yes, straight, no turns." Jerriney nodded. They went into the tunnel and started walking underground towards the kitchen.

"Some of the guards will be going to the village and others will still be waking up. I don't think you will have any trouble getting to the mage's room. If you can, make sure his door is locked. If possible, use your magic to make it unbreakable. Once men hear fighting, I'm sure they will rush to help their master. The mage usually studies over his books in the morning so you might be able to slip in and surprise him."

"Okay, thank you." They had entered the kitchen.

"There is the hallway." The cook pointed towards a small hall that was only wide enough for one person.

She gently grabbed Jerriney by the shoulders. "Be careful. Do not give him any room to attack. Do not hesitate. Be confident in whatever you do. This whole village believes in you Jerriney. Remember that."

"Alright, I'll remember that. I really appreciate your help," Jerriney replied. She headed into the small hall that would lead her to the end of this journey. She tried not to be nervous and focused on thinking of how she could use her magic in ways that might help her in the upcoming fight.

It didn't take long until the hallway ended. Jerriney carefully peeked out of the passage to make sure there weren't any guards. The woman was right, no one was about. To Jerriney's right were a flight of stairs. She couldn't tell how long they went on because they winded up.

"Of course, the evil man's room has to be all the way up in the tall tower," Jerriney commented out loud to herself.

Jerriney started ascending the staircase. She tried not to make any noise, but the further up she went, the more tired she got and her footsteps began to fall heavier. Then she had an idea, *"Maybe I can use magic to muffle my steps."* She stopped a moment and closed her eyes. She summoned her magic and envisioned it circling around her feet. Once she thought she had done it, she took a step. Nothing. Her foot made no noise. She tried again, this time stomping her foot. Still nothing. She smiled at herself, pleased that it hadn't taken her very long. Jerriney continued up the stairs with renewed confidence. She felt like she could do anything she put her mind to.

𝔉𝔦𝔰𝔥𝔢𝔯 went straight to the inn. The rest of the travelers had not yet awoken, so he helped his brother's wife make breakfast. Soon enough their guests started trickling in. They served them as they came. Once they were all gathered and were almost done eating, someone finally said something.

"Where's Jerriney?" Drust asked.

Rhonwen looked around, pausing to glare at Muirnen. He got up and rushed to her room. Her bed was folded neatly and all her things were in place. He returned to the rest of the group.

"She's not in her room. There's no sign of a struggle," he reported to the group.

"Maybe she went for a walk," Nicodemus offered.

"No, she didn't go for a walk," Fisher said. They all looked at him.

242

"She came to my house early this morning. She insisted I take her to the citadel. If I didn't help her, she'd go in anyway. I sent her with the cook. She would have been killed if I hadn't helped her."

They were silent for a while.

"I had a feeling she'd do something like that," Rhonwen said.

"She told me that she did want you to follow her in though. You should leave as soon as possible. Jerriney just wants to fight the mage herself," Fisher told them.

"Alright. Let's hurry up and finish here. We'll leave right away," Rhonwen commanded as he left the table.

It felt like ages before Jerriney reached the top of the stairs. She sat down to rest so that she would not go in with a heavy breath. Her rest was short lived. Not long after she sat down, she heard voices and footsteps coming up the stairs. She stood up. There were no other doors at the top of this tower so her choices were go in now, or fight whoever was coming up. Thankfully, she didn't have to make that choice. Right when she saw the shadows they stopped.

"Ay, you 'ear that?" said one of the men. It was

243

quiet as they listened.

"Yea! Someone's shoutin'!" said the other man.

They hurried back down the stairs.

"That must be Rhonwen and the rest of the group. I need to fight that mage now!" Jerriney said to herself. She turned to the door. "Please don't be squeaky."

† Chapter Twenty-One †

Jerriney slowly turned the knob to the mage's door. She gently pushed on the wooden door. Once it was open enough for her to fit through, she peeked her head around. There was a man sitting at a desk hunched over a book with his back to her, right in line of the door. He didn't move. Jerriney slipped through. She was glad to find out the door did not swing back. She didn't want to try and quietly close it, even though the cook told her to lock it, for fear it would click and rouse the mage from his studies.

There were shelves full of books on all of the mage's walls, except the wall his bed was against. She looked quickly for where the stones might be.

"Maybe I can get the stones and leave without any confrontation." Jerriney hoped to herself. She didn't move as she looked around the room. She didn't have to look far to find what she was seeking. On one of the shelves there was a small, linen satchel with blue stones spilling out. It was to the right of Jerriney and the mage.

Jerriney slowly inched towards the stones. She was

worried that they were in his peripheral vision. She was almost in reach of them.

"I hope you do not actually think I did not know you came in," said the mage calmly.

Jerriney gasped and took a step back. Her back was against a bookshelf. The mage stood up and looked at her.

"I have known you were here since you stepped on the landing at the top of the stairs." He got out of his chair and took a step to his right. Jerriney did so as well.

"If you knew I was here, why didn't you do anything?" She took another step to the right.

The mage laughed as he shadowed her move. "You are harmless. Your magic seeps out of you. Clearly you do not have control of it."

"You don't know what I'm capable of. I almost killed your man the other day. Hardly took me anything to do it," Jerriney said. She felt for her magic so she would have it right away. She kept slowly edging to the right. She hoped that if he was in front of the door then if anyone rushed in they would run into him and throw him off. He continued to copy her as she moved.

"Ha! That was because you had absolutely no control! You could have killed yourself, or worse, your friends."

Jerriney drew her sword.

"You think this is a sword fight? I'm the most powerful mage in the world. You think a little piece of metal can defeat me?"

The mage was now in front of the door and Jerriney found herself beside some kind of orb. The stand it was on had a dark, sinister look. It was black and had thick spikes ornately jutting out all over. She hated to think what he might do with the orb. She had heard of the many things orbs can do—spy on people, trap people. She hoped she was not in danger standing near it.

"Alright, here's how we'll do this," said the mage as he clasped his hands, his long sleeves nearly concealing them from view. "Since you are so young and inexperienced, I'll go easy on you. I'll attack you with my powers, and then I'll give you a turn to attack in any way you want. It'll be like a game! Doesn't it sound fun?"

"Get on with it. I don't have time for your games," Jerriney responded. She was worried, but she tried not to show it.

"Ha! Ha ha!" The mage laughed. "Ready, little girl?" he said as he brought his arms back and then he forced his right hand forward as if he was pushing something at Jerriney.

She quickly put her left arm up, palm facing him, as she tugged on her magic and imagined a strong, unbreakable wall in front of her. She felt the force of his magic as it hit her invisible shield. Jerriney struggled not to let go of her hold on the magic.

Before the mage attacked again she threw a ball of magic which, to her surprise, was blue, at the mage's face. He caught it inches before his nose with his Dark Magic, black outlining Jerriney's blue, and instantly forced it back at her. This time Jerriney did not react soon enough to block it. It hit her left shoulder and she stumbled to the right, bumping into the stand that the mysterious orb was on. The orb fell to the ground and Jerriney watched it roll under the bed.

The mage snickered at Jerriney and walked to his right, pretending to inspect the book shelves for dust.

"Child, I have not even begun to try. Nothing you can do will harm me." The mage smiled and turned to Jerriney. He put his hands together in front of him then he slowly pulled them apart. As his hands moved further and further away, Jerriney could see a shape forming. His arms were spread all the way out. He had formed a magical black spear. Jerriney dropped her sword and willed her magic to her hands. The mage thrust his arms forward sending the spear right towards Jerriney. She quickly grabbed the pole of the spear, stopping it before it reached her. She was glad the mage had done a similar thing with her attack when she threw a magic ball at him for she probably would not have thought of that herself. This was her first fight with magic so she did not know all that she was able to do.

The spear disappeared in her hands. The mage laughed again. Jerriney noticed something ominous seemed to be slowly leaking out of him, pulling on his very essence. It looked like oily clouds as it traveled under the bed. The mage manifested a black throwing star and threw it at Jerriney. She side-stepped it and, using her magic, picked up a nearby book and forced it towards his stomach as hard as she could. It hit the man hard and he doubled over. He coughed and struggled to catch his breath.

More black clouds came out of him and it seemed as if he was aging quickly.

"What's happening?" said the mage as he looked at his wrinkling hands. "My magic, I-I can't find it!"

The blackness rushed out of him now. His hair grew longer and turned white, his body thinned to where you could see his every bone and his clothes seemed too big. He fell to his knees as he continued to lose his powers. Jerriney picked up her sword and walked up to him. She kneeled and looked into his eyes. His once dark as midnight eyes were now a brilliant green, but quickly faded into grey.

"Where am I? Who are you?" he slowly said in the voice of a withered old man.

"You're in your room. Do you know who you are?" Jerriney asked him.

He looked around and then brought his focus back to Jerriney. His eyes looked terribly sad.

"My name is Marwin," he said as his skin started to sag.

𝕽honwen, Drust, and Muirnen had gone in the front of the citadel, fighting those that opposed them. They noticed that some men sank into the shadows, as if they did not care what was happening.

Draxx, Nicodemus, Nazema, and Melanthious found a way in through the back. Here, there weren't as many guards for them to fight. They quickly arrived at the stairway that lead to the mage's room. They bolted up the stairs. When they got to the top there were six men waiting for them.

"The Master's in a fight right now. You can 'ave your go at 'em when he's finished with the girl," said a man in the front.

Draxx said nothing, but drew his sword as he continued rushing towards the guard that spoke. He drove his blade deep into the man's stomach and pushed him away, jumping to the next guard.

Nazema rushed passed and went for one of the men in the back. She lunged her sword at him, but he blocked it. He pulled out second sword and started a series of attacks on her. Nazema worked hard to block attacks from both swords, but she was not as experienced as the other Shifters and soon became tired. The man was pushing her backwards and she fell to the ground. He raised one of his swords to strike her.

"Draxx!" she screamed. He rushed to her aid and plunged his sword into the man's back. The others had already subdued the rest of the guards and turned to look at her.

"Did Nazema just yell?" Melanthious asked.

𝔍errinep watched, horrified as the mage's flesh melted off, exposing his muscles. The mage let out a bloodcurdling scream as he continued to decompose.

His muscles dried up and fell, turning to ash as they hit the ground. Jerriney dropped her sword as she stood and backed away as the mage's heart pounded against his ribs, bleeding from the cuts the bones made. She looked away and closed her eyes until the man, who now looked more like a monster, ceased to scream. Jerriney dared to look at him. She watched his bare skeleton fall to the ground and burst into grey flakes. All that was left of the Dark Mage was a pile of ash.

Suddenly her friends poured into the room. They stopped abruptly when they saw Jerriney standing awe-struck in front of a pile of dust.

"What happened?" Nicodemus questioned Jerriney. "Where is the mage?"

"We were fighting with magic and he about had me, but I bumped into that stand over there." She pointed to the black, ornate stand that was now lying on the floor. "There was an orb on it and it rolled off somewhere. I think it had something to do with the Dark Magic because black smoke started coming out of the mage and he lost his powers. Then he started aging rapidly until his flesh melted off and his muscles and organs became dust." Jerriney's voice became hoarse and she began to cry. "And then his skeleton started deteriorating until it became this!" Jerriney said as she gestured at the pile of ashes.

"That must have been how Nazema got her voice back!" Nicodemus exclaimed, ignoring the gory scene Jerriney just described.

"Nazema can speak?" Drust looked at her quizzically.

"I can now." She smiled at him.

"How does that work?" Drust inquired.

"Well, if the orb was the source of his Dark Magic, he probably had a portal being held open in the glass. He was the mage that we saved Nazema from, but he took her voice. While the orb was taking away the mage's powers, it must have undone the spell that he had cast on Nazema, returning her voice," Nicodemus explained.

"That's great!" Jerriney said as she went up and hugged Nazema.

"Let's go back to the village and tell them what happened," Rhonwen told the group.

"Before the mage started screaming he said his name was Marwin. Maybe some of the villagers knew him before he was corrupted by Dark Magic and can tell us his story," Jerriney said as she grabbed the stones that held the remaining seven trapped dragons' souls.

Nicodemus went over to the bed and grabbed a

blanket off it. He bent over and reached under the bed, grabbed the orb with the blanket and wrapped it tightly.

Jerriney and her friends left the citadel and told the villagers what had happened.

𝕯ashlegar was headed up through a secret passage to speak to the mage. Dark Magic had sped up his healing tremendously so he was able to walk around, but it still pained him. He had just arrived at the secret door in the mage's room when he heard a young woman's voice. He stopped and cast a spell on the door so that he could see through it, but no one in the room could see him.

To his right, Jerriney stood in front of the actual door. The mage was standing opposite her. He looked like he had it under control so Dashlegar stayed behind the hidden door. Dashlegar also was in no condition to fight so he had no intention of helping this man. Sure, Dashlegar was working for him, but he would get his reward whether or not the mage won this fight.

Dashlegar watched in silence as the two figures began battling with magic. Surprisingly, it did not take long for the fighting to end. By chance, Jerriney had bumped into the source of the mage's powers. Dashlegar saw it roll under the bed as it started taking back the mage's Dark Magic.

Once the mage was no more, Dashlegar continued to watch as Jerriney told her companions what happened. He paid close attention when one of them went and retrieved the orb from under the bed.

"Well I can't let them have such a powerful item. I could make great use of it," Dashlegar thought to himself.

Once Jerriney finished recalling her story to the villagers, she went to talk to Fisher.

"Does the name Marwin mean anything to you?" Jerriney asked Fisher while the villagers talked to the rest of her companions.

Fisher thought for a while, stroking the stubble on his chin. "You know, it does sound oddly familiar," he said. "I bet old Marge would know. She's the oldest in this town and is the widow of our late historian. He left all his books in their basement and she spent a lot of time reading over them to keep his spirit with her."

"C'mon," Fisher said as he motioned for Jerriney to follow. "I'll bring you to her. She doesn't leave her

255

house anymore."

Jerriney motioned to find her friends. "I'll be right back." She followed Fisher through the town.

"𝕸arwin?" The old lady Marge paused. "Oh yes! He was a spirited young fellow," she told Jerriney. "At least, that's what the history books say. One of the books my husband left behind told of how charming Marwin was. He used his magic to help people with their troubles. It seems as though everyone loved him." She looked at Jerriney. "He was very interested in studying magic. I bet he read every book ever written on the subject. Unfortunately, that also included Dark Magic, which became his downfall. No one knows exactly what happened to him, but it was rumored that he opened a demonic portal and was sucked in. He hasn't been seen since, which is actually quite sad." Marge sighed and looked at a cricket that had jumped on her shoe.

"Thank you, that was very helpful." Jerriney smiled at her.

"Before you go," Marge started, "would you mind telling me what peeked your interest in Marwin?"

"Well," Jerriney paused, "before the Dark Man

became ash, he mentioned Marwin. I don't know what he was talking about though," Jerriney fibbed. The memory of Marwin was so pleasant that she didn't want to taint it with the fact that he became the man who tormented the people of this village.

Jerriney thanked Marge again and returned with Fisher to the villagers and her friends.

There was pie on the table and the people looked happier then when Jerriney had first come to this little town. The villagers gathered around her when she entered the room. They were overjoyed to see her again and wanted to once again convey their gratitude.

The stout cook came up to Jerriney and gave her a big hug. "You'll never know how much we appreciate you and your friends." Jerriney's face was turning red from being squeezed so hard by the large lady.

"You are most welcome," Jerriney said as she was released. It felt good to have saved such nice people from the Dark Mage.

Once Jerriney and her friends finished speaking with the villagers, Fisher cooked them something to eat. They decided that once they were done eating they would go straight to the tomb and return the rest of the souls. Jerriney was excited to see what would happen next. They had nearly accomplished their goals. The

Dark Mage was defeated, all twelve souls would soon be reunited with the dragons, and they had saved many people in the process. Out of all the people she saved from the mage's torment, she felt this small village was most important. It had been under his tyranny for so long, they hadn't even seen the rest of Amensdale! These people had so much to learn about the world they lived in.

† Chapter Twenty-Two †

Raleigh Criterious was kneading dough when she felt a breeze enter the kitchen. She turned around to see where it was coming from.

"Hello, Raleigh," said a busty woman in a malevolent tone. She was wearing a red gown with gold accents that seemed to fade at her feet.

"W-who are you? What are you doing here?" Raleigh queried.

"You're Jerriney's mother yes?" The woman stepped towards Raleigh.

"How did you get that name? There's only one person I told about her," Raleigh replied as she backed away.

"I've been looking for you for a long time, Raleigh. You're a hard person to find, you know that?" She picked up a piece of dough from the table and rolled it in her fingers.

"What are you talking about? What do you want from me?" Raleigh was frantically looking for a weapon with her hands behind her back.

The mysterious woman flicked the dough behind

her. "I'm here to kill you," she simply stated.

Raleigh shrank back in fear. "Why would you want to do that?" She looked around her for an escape.

"You are the mortal that carried my god's, disgusting half-mortal child. No one but me can have the love of Baldemor Dahkni, God of War! Because of you, he missed the birth of his son! Now I shall get my revenge, and Baldemor will no longer come to earth."

"I, I'm sorry! He didn't tell me he had a goddess at home. Please, it's not my fault!" Raleigh pleaded. "He came to me! He should be the one to punish."

"Stupid mortal. A goddess never harms her god. This would not have happened if you did not exist. It's all your fault." She pulled out an ivory dagger that was magically poisoned and approached Raleigh.

"Please, don't! I'm begging you. Please!"

"Know that the goddess Variter Rose will be the Bringer of Death for you and your daughter." She plunged the dagger once into Raleigh's chest, piercing her heart. The poison instantly spread through her entire body, killing her right away. The goddess left Raleigh with the dagger in her heart.

𝕵erriney and the others returned to the tomb to give the rest of the souls back to the dragons. They had entered the tomb and Jerriney stood in the middle like she had done before. She reached into her pouch, took out the seven blue stones, and placed them on the floor. She took a step back and waited. After a while the stones flew to their respective skeletons as the first five had. She expected the skeletons to come alive at once, like last time, but something else happened instead.

They felt the air change. It went from damp and stuffy to feeling like they were out in the fresh air. Suddenly, the wall that blocked them from the outside world started to disappear. It started in the middle; a small hole appeared and grew larger and larger until they were standing in front of green grass and butterflies flying to and from the many flowers.

A gloom had been over Amensdale for centuries, like a storm cloud. Now, as the tomb opened up to blue skies and cheerful birds, so did the rest of the land. The darkness lifted and everything became vibrant. The whole world seemed to be joyful of the return of the High Dragons.

The dragons' bones that were under a spell that kept them from decaying now turned to dust and sailed away on the light breeze. The five souls that Jerriney

261

had already returned jubilantly swarmed around the new stones.

Jerriney stepped outside. The rest followed close behind. She looked back in the cave and watched the souls come out of each stone and join their fellow dragon souls. They rushed out to Jerriney. The souls swirled around the group like young birds just gaining their wings, and freedom with it. Then the souls meshed together in front of Jerriney to form an astral dragon, so huge Jerriney had to look almost straight up to see its head.

"The twelve High Dragons thank you for freeing us Jerriney," the voices of the twelve High Dragons came together to speak at once.

"You are welcome," Jerriney said in awe.

"And thank you, friends of Jerriney; Shifters and humans coming together to save the dragons, two very different creatures usually not fond of each other. And the offspring of a god as well! Yours is a story that will last for centuries," said the celestial dragon.

The Shifters humbly bowed and Muirnen and Drust followed their lead once they realized what was happening.

"The High Dragons can now be reborn, and the race of dragons can start again. The mage who brought the destruction of our race is dead. No longer will dragons hide in fear. With their leaders among them, they will once again take to the skies! Our only hope is that humans do not do as their ancestors did, and hunt us down. As our saviors, we hope that the eight of you will spread the word and educate those you meet. Tell them we are a peaceful race and do not wish for the battle between humans and dragons to continue." The formed dragon lowered its head so it was eye level to Jerriney.

"We will tell everyone we meet to look to the skies for friends, not enemies," Jerriney remarked, beaming with joy that she had done what she had come to do and saved the dragon race in the process.

The dragon looked to the Shifters. "And we hope that you may find your place in this world as well, not being hunted by the humans. Together we can join to make this land peaceful as it once was before the gods meddled in our affairs. We must leave now, it will take many years for us to find the perfect egg and be reborn."

"Before you leave," Jerriney started as she took the dragon tear from her pouch, "I have this dragon tear that I found before this journey when I was hunting. I give it back to those it belongs to." She held her hand out in front of her.

"Keep it. It will help you harness your own power and strengthen you in times of need. Consider it as a gift."

"Thank you," Jerriney said to the dragon manifestation as she bowed in respect.

The High Dragons' souls then separated and formed twelve separate dragons and flew up into the sky, each their own color. They lingered above Jerriney and her friends for a while as a gesture to say thank you again and then departed separate ways, like the spokes of a wagon wheel.

"I don't even know what to say," Drust broke the silence.

"That was amazing," Muirnen uttered.

"I have never seen anything as beautiful as that, and I have lived a very, very long time," Nicodemus said as he wiped a tear from the corner of his eye.

"What do we do now?" Jerriney asked as she looked around.

"I don't know. Everything seems so boring compared to what we have experienced in the past few weeks," Rhonwen commented as he lifted his finger gently in the air to let a butterfly land.

"Well I want to go back to Bar'diin," Nicodemus

announced. "I miss being around Sully and since she is no longer with us, I think Bar'diin would be a good dragon."

"Someone say my name?" Bar'diin's words rumbled through everyone as he suddenly appeared. He landed in front of the group. *"I felt something stir deep inside of me and I knew that Jerriney had succeeded. I followed that feeling here in hopes I could meet the High Dragons."*

"You just missed them," Jerriney told the white dragon.

"A shame," Bar'diin hung his head in sadness. *"For so long have I dreamt of meeting our leaders, but this is a time of rejoicing! I still may yet get to see them one day as they are no longer enslaved. You do not know how much joy this brings me, Jerriney, how much joy you have brought to my dying race."* He looked her in the eyes and she thought she saw tears.

"I am humbled by your gratitude, Bar'diin. I could not have done it without your help. If you hadn't trusted us and told me where the dragons' shrine was, we would still be searching." Jerriney put a hand on the side of his maw.

"Where will you all go from here? I know you are all far from home. If any of you need, I can fly you

somewhere," Bar'diin offered as he raised his head.

"I'd like to return to the village," Muirnen said. "I came down to earth with harsh thoughts against the human race. Traveling with this group has given me a change of heart. I wish to help the villagers of Sudar get back on their feet. With the Dark Mage gone, they will need a strong leader who will guide them into the rest of the world and not lead them astray."

"That is very noble of you. It is not something you would expect from the gods. You certainly have changed my view of your people, Muirnen," Bar'diin told him. *"Maybe not all gods and their offspring are arrogant fools."*

"Nicodemous would like to join you by the ocean, Bar'diin. Nazema, Melanthious and I would like to go as well," Draxx told the dragon.

"That is fine with me. I have been in seclusion for so long I have forgotten the joy of company."

"I'd like to join also," Rhonwen stepped forward. "I have lived so much of my life as a housecat, and although I enjoyed my time with you Jerriney, I should like to learn the ways of my people, and who better to learn it from then some of the oldest alive."

"I think that's a good idea," Jerriney said and smiled at him. "I'd like to go home. I don't know what

I'll find there, but Loreen is still there. She'll help me."

"I don't think I can carry more than three. Nazema is small so I might be able to take you four Shifters. I would have to come back for Jerriney and Rhonwen."

"Sounds like a plan," Draxx said.

"Shall we leave right away? Before it gets dark?" Nicodemus asked.

"That's fine with me," Draxx replied.

"Hold on," Jerriney said. "What happens to the orb?

"We will take it with us," Draxx told her.

"It needs to be destroyed, but that task is much harder than it sounds. We have to make sure we properly seal the portal or else demons will escape," Nicodemus explained.

"That sounds like a good plan. If I can help in any way, I am more than willing," Jerriney told them as they climbed onto Bar'diin's back. They waved goodbye as the great, white dragon took to the skies and headed to the ocean caves.

"Drust!" Jerriney exclaimed shortly after Bar'diin took off. "You didn't say what you are to do now. Where will you go?"

"Well, I honestly don't know. I don't have any family and I don't want to go back and work for that crude blacksmith." Drust nudged a twig with his foot. What he wouldn't tell Jerriney is that he really just wanted to stay with her. Fortunately he didn't have to.

"You could come back with me. My aunt and uncle were killed in that ambush and I was living with Ron and Liz who are dead now as well. I wouldn't mind having someone to keep me company. Plus, I think it would be nice having someone to talk to who has experienced all this with me, and I've grown quite fond of your company." Jerriney smiled.

"Really? You would let me come with you?" Drust's eyes lit up.

Jerriney smiled. "Yes, of course."

Drust ran up and embraced her in a warm hug.

Muirnen started walking back to the town.

"Hold up, Muirnen. I'd like to speak with you," Rhonwen said as he ran after him. They continued walking as he spoke.

"I know I never really trusted you, Muirnen, but you turned out to be a faithful companion. I am sorry I ever doubted you."

"There is no need to thank me. My intentions were not always kind."

"What do you mean?" Rhonwen asked. Muirnen stopped walking.

"I was sent here to find out who Jerriney's mother was. My mother is a goddess called Variter Rose and wanted to kill Jerriney's mother. I didn't know that when I first came here." Muirnen looked at a bird building a nest.

"You see, my father, who is also Jerriney's father, came to Amensdale one day and met a human. She was very beautiful and he spent a long time with her. During that time, I was born. Variter was very angry that he had missed my birth. Years passed and he returned. My mom had already sent me to find the woman he was with so I have never met him." He looked back at Rhonwen.

"When Jerriney was born my mother felt it since she is a goddess of fertility, and she also sensed Jerriney's immortal blood. She sent me after her since I could find her easier because Variter cannot sense where mortals are, only their babies. Last I spoke to my mother, she had found Jerriney's mother and was going to kill her. She told me to kill Jerriney. I almost did too, because I didn't want to disappoint my mother, but I have become too fond of Jerriney. What my mother did was not right. I decided to return to the village because

I do not think my mother will allow me back home."
Muirnen finished with a stern look on his face.

"That is very shocking to hear. I am glad you did
not listen to your mother, Muirnen. Know that I will
always think highly of you. You have vanquished the
evil in yourself that is in everyone, that the Dark Mage
we just faced could not. You should be proud of
yourself." Rhonwen smiled at Muirnen. "You will be a
good leader to the people of Sudar." He hugged him
and returned to Jerriney and Drust.

Rhonwen decided to keep what he had learned to
himself for now. Jerriney did not need to know things
of the past that she could not, and never did, have
control over. He was sure she would someday find out
about her mother, but right now was a time for
celebration not weeping over a mother she never knew.

Muirnen looked at the ground as he walked to the
village. He wished his mother had not used him against
the people he now considered his friends. He wondered
what it would have been like if he had joined them on
friendly terms rather than being a spy for his mother.

"Did you do it?" A voice startled him out of his
thoughts.

Muirnen looked up to find his mother standing in front of him, wearing a red gown.

"Did I do what?" he muttered and continued walking on.

She grabbed his arm. "Kill the girl! I told you to kill the girl! I just finished with her mother. We can go home now, if you killed her."

"I didn't kill her," he firmly stated.

"What? Why not?" She looked at him, puzzled.

"It is not your right to decide who dies and when they die. Jerriney did nothing wrong and as far as I'm concerned and neither did her mother. It's the father that is to blame. Baldemor is the one you should have been taking your revenge out on."

"Don't be silly child. The girl is still here. Go kill her quick and we can be off," his mother insisted.

"No, I'm not going to kill her and neither are you. She deserves to live more than you do!" Muirnen spat at his mother. She let go of his arm and stumbled back in shock.

"How dare you speak to your mother like that! I've given you everything you have! I've nurtured you since you were but a babe!"

"You've done none of that!" Muirnen yelled at her. "You barely even know me! All I am to you is a pawn to use in your next great plan. Well I've got news for you mother, I'm not coming home with you. I'm not going to listen to you ever again. I make my own decisions. I will live my own life, not a life governed by you." He spun around and returned to walking toward the village.

"I will not stand for this treachery! Know that you are banned from ever coming home, Muirnen!" Variter yelled after him.

It didn't take long for Bar'diin to return for Jerriney, Rhonwen, and Drust. He dropped Rhonwen off with the other Shifters first, and then flew to Jerriney's home in Ascillia. He landed a ways out of town so no one would spot him. Jerriney and Drust walked in silence to Jerriney's house, both lost in their own thoughts.

Jerriney was so deep in her mind that she wasn't looking where she was going, just following the familiar footsteps, when she stepped in something that shouldn't have been there. Black debris. She looked up.

"What's this?" she said as she looked around the area that should have held Ron and Liz's house.

"It looks like someone burned something here,"

Drust said.

"My house is supposed to be here! This is where I spent most of my life growing up! Who would have burned it?" Jerriney started crying as she remembered all the times spent with Ron and Liz, all the things that were in the house that held sentimental value to her. All she had now was the clothes on her back and the sword at her side.

"That's terrible," Drust said and took her in his arms to comfort her.

After several moments past, the sky started getting darker and thunder could be heard off in the distance.

"It's getting dark and I think there's a storm coming in. We need to get to shelter. Do you know a place where we can stay?" Drust asked Jerriney.

"We can go to Loreen," she simply said and grabbed his hand to lead the way.

When they arrived at Loreen's house the sun had set and they had only the moon to guide them. Clouds were blocking out the stars and it was starting to sprinkle. Jerriney knocked on the door.

"Who is it, banging on my door so late?" They heard Loreen yelling at the door. Jerriney smiled as she

273

remembered her old friend. The door opened.

"Jerriney?" Loreen squinted in the limited light. "It is! Jerriney! Come, come in before it starts pouring! Who is your friend?"

"This is Drust. He helped me on my journey. He was working at a blacksmith, but he doesn't want to go back. He has no family and since I don't either now, I thought he could stay with me in Ron and Liz's house and keep me company, but I went there and it's burnt down!" Tears formed in Jerriney's eyes again. "Everything's gone."

"Oh dearie, come here." Loreen beckoned her forward so she could comfort her with a hug.

"I know what happened to your house." Loreen held her in front of her. "I was gathering herbs near Ron and Liz's house. I heard voices so I went to see what was going on. I thought maybe you had come home. I started over that hill that's so darn steep, and saw that it was not you. It was some man with a goblin and several other men. The one guy was yelling at the others and he ordered them to burn it. Then they left." Loreen began to lead them through her house.

"I would have tried to put the fire out, but I would have needed help and the village is too far away for an old woman like me and it was a rather warm day. But! I did go in around the back and I saved one of your old teddy bears. I believe it's the one Ron gave you when you first joined their family." Loreen stopped walking to smile at Jerriney.

"Thank you for risking your life and getting the bear. I'm glad I still have something to remember them by."

"Oh! And I have more news! A couple of strangers came up to my door the other day and I have them over for tea right now! They would very much like to see you."

Jerriney had no clue what this crazy lady was talking about, but she followed her anyway.

"You come too Drust boy!" Loreen called behind her.

Jerriney walked around the corner and sitting around Loreen's fireplace were John and Tesa.

"What?" Jerriney said, confounded. "But, you're dead! What happened?" She ran up to them as they stood and hugged them.

"It was a staged ambush by Dashlegar. I suspect he was the same man that burned Ron's house," John told her.

"Come sit dear, you've grown so much since we last saw you," Tesa said. Jerriney sat beside her. Her aunt took her face in her hands and brushed her hair back. "You've become such a beautiful young lady." She smiled at Jerriney and a tear formed in the corner of her eye.

"Thank you, Tesa." Jerriney smiled. "Tell me more about what happened," Jerriney asked, eager to hear of their adventure.

"Alright, but then you have to tell us about your journey too." Tesa had Jerriney sit beside her and beckoned Drust to come sit as well.

"Before you begin," Loreen interrupted. "I need to inform Jerriney of our other visitor."

"Oh, yes! Yes, go on," John said rather excitedly.

"Jerriney, you have another uncle who is here. He came today from the Abbey up by Duvok so he was very tired and is sleeping right now, but he has something he would like to tell you. He is a monk called Demeter."

Jerriney was shocked. Demeter was the monk they were looking for when she started her journey! She wanted to say something, but John pulled her out of her thoughts.

"We were headed home ..." John started. He recalled how they fought on the ship with Dashlegar's goblins until they were overcome and then taken to an island. He described in great detail the Dwarven halls hidden in the caves and how they brought scrolls back for Loreen. John even mentioned that one day they might go back, the three of them, Loreen if she was up to it and Drust too, to explore the halls. Then he told how Dashlegar didn't even care that they escaped. They went with him on the ship to Kodar Docks along with one of the king's other men that had survived. From there they snuck off and found some horses. Gozan, the other man that had survived, went on to report to the king. John stated how surprised he was that it was so easy to get away and that Dashlegar was obviously focused on getting the stones. From there they came straight home. They were distressed when they found Ron and Liz's burnt house and went to Loreen who told them where Jerriney was and that Ron had gone with her and that Liz died of a strange illness not too long before they left.

"So, where is Ron?" Tesa asked.

Jerriney bowed her head. "He died saving me. We were ambushed while resting one night. Ron was getting wood for the fire so he saw them before the rest of us knew they were there. One of the men we were ambushed by took a shot at me with his bow. Ron jumped right in front of the arrow, and died not long afterward. After the fight was over, my friends looked through their things, and that's when we found out I was being targeted by Dashlegar," Jerriney told them.

"Speaking of missing persons, where is Nerezzan?" Loreen asked. Jerriney had to think who Nerezzan was for a short while. She was so used to calling him Rhonwen that she forgot he used to be called Nerezzan.

"Oh! Um, Rhonwen." Jerriney looked at Loreen to see if she knew what she was talking about. Loreen smiled at her and nodded her head, signaling that she knew he was a Shifter. "He is safe. We met some other Shifters on our travels and he decided to go with them. He said they were ancient and said he wanted to learn more about his people. I know where he went so we can visit him whenever, although it is quite a ways away."

"Oh that is alright child. I just wanted to make sure he was still alive and well," Loreen said, waving off the thought of traveling miles away.

"Now tell us your story, Jerriney. I'm eager to learn how you met Drust here, and how you defeated Dashlegar. We are so proud of you, Jerriney," Tesa told her and smiled.

"Well, when I got your stones …" Jerriney spent the rest of the evening and well into the night recalling her journey and how she battled in her first fights and discovered her magic and spoke with dragons. She described the mystical Dragons' Shrine and how magnificent dragons looked in person. Drust told about his favorite part, the dragon skeletons coming to life and Jerriney in the middle of it all.

Jerriney had not remembered when she had been this happy. She had finally gone on an adventure of her own and it looked like there was more to come. She had lost those she loved dearly, but she gained those she thought were dead and learned so much on her journey. She felt she should be celebrating their lives, not grieving over it. Jerriney had saved Amensdale and those she held dear, spoke with the dying race of dragons, fought beside the misunderstood Shifters, and learned there is more to a person then what meets the eye. She could not wait to tell future generations her story.

In the morning, Jerriney's new-found uncle, the monk Demeter, told her something she did not expect. Her mother, whom she did not know existed, had been killed by an unknown person. When he went to visit her, like he so often did, he found an empty house. He went on to ask the neighbors if they knew where his sister was. They told him she had been found in her house on the ground, an ivory dagger plunged in her heart. Strangely, she looked just as she was when she was alive, the pink still shown in her skin. Since she looked so beautiful, the neighbors decided to craft her a glass coffin and be placed in a tomb, so that her beauty could be displayed for eternity. Demeter said that if Jerriney wished, she could go and visit her sometime.

Jerriney said she would like to do that as soon as possible.

Demeter also mentioned that, among his sister's things, he found a note. On it explained why John and Tesa had the blue stones in the first place.

Many, many years ago, a Shifter with powers of foresight gathered up the stones that were not in possession of the evil mage. He gave them to one of John and Raleigh's ancestors and was told that the stones should be passed down to every daughter of the Criterious family and that one day, one of the daughters would need the stones to save Amensdale.

Demeter said that his sister had given John the stones because he was to raise Jerriney. She had hoped that if Jerriney was not with her, the wrath of her father's goddess would not spread to Jerriney. Demeter did not know why the note was not with the stones.

Jerriney held the dragon tear in her hand the entire day, eager to explore the limits of her powers. She thought about her mother, whom she found out was named Raleigh, and she thought about Bar'diin and Sully. She was glad that soon she could look to the sky and watch the dragons fly majestically overhead. There was so much more she needed to learn and she felt as if the prophecies would one day lead her on a new adventure.

† Epilogue †

Variter Rose walked diligently to the front of the Council. She had been summoned by the High Gods to account for her actions on Earth.

"Variter Rose," boomed the High God of Judgment. "You have been accused of disobeying our predecessors by traveling to the human's realm, using your own kin to do your meddling, and killing one of their women out of spite. Do you deny these accusations?"

The goddess looked over at the High God of War. "No. You have been told correctly." She glared at Baldemor.

"For your thoughtless actions, and previous behavior towards other gods and goddesses, the Council of the High Gods has unanimously agreed that you are to be banned from our realm and will spend the rest of your life with the humans, as a human."

Variter's eyes bulged. "What? You can't do that! Baldemor, tell them they can't do this," she demanded.

"We have spoken," replied the council. "Take her

away!"

 Once Dashlegar was fully healed, he used his dark magic to spy on Nicodemus. He wanted to see what he would do with the orb. Thankfully, Dashlegar did not get his dark magic from the orb like the dark mage had, so he had lost nothing in the events of the past. With his magic, he found out that Nicodemus and the rest of the Shifters went to live by the ocean, taking the orb with them. Dashlegar noted their location and went to plan how he would take the orb for himself one day.

 When Muirnen arrived back at the village of Sudar he went to Fisher to tell him of his idea. Fisher thought it was a great plan and immediately called a village meeting. Everyone agreed that they needed help putting their village back together and learning the new traditions of the world.

Muirnen began his role as leader of the village by bringing in scholars and teachers and changing the citadel into a place where people could learn about Amensdale and how it had changed over the years.

Once the villagers were up to date about the land beyond their mountains, Muirnen led them to other cities and as their story spread, the village became a tourist attraction and grew into wealth.

One day, Fisher came up to Muirnen and mentioned that the people would like to change the town's name, as a way to celebrate their freedom from the Dark Man. They chose to use the name that the town had been called centuries ago, Allur.

And now, a glimpse at Naomi's next book

Reign of Kaos

Melanthious sat alone by the fire in the cave they had been living in for the past couple months. Draxx, Nazema, Rhonwen, and Nicodemus had gone with the white dragon Bar'diin to search for a hermit who supposedly had important information.

The five Shifters had recently helped a young demi-god return the souls of the High Dragons to their skeletons, thus giving them a chance to be reborn and guide the dragons as they recovered their endangered race. It was an evil human mage who had trapped them. The young demi-god, Jerriney, and her friends promised to spread the word that dragons were a peaceful race and not to be hunted. Hopefully this would save the dragons from going extinct.

Melanthious prodded the fire. He enjoyed going with Bar'diin when they flew to find more of his kind and he loved meeting more dragons, but all five Shifters could not go every time. One always had to stay and guard the orb. It had belonged to the evil mage who had trapped the High Dragons' souls so it was highly important that it did not fall into the wrong hands. Of course, the shape-shifters did not expect anyone to try and steal the orb. They had rid all who knew of it, or so they thought.

Dashlegar crept towards the cave the shape-shifters were living in. He saw most of them leave a few minutes ago. It looked like they would be gone for a while. He had been watching them from his hideout in the Promoka Mountains. Dashlegar had spied on them using his Dark Magic from afar because if he were closer to the powerful shape-shifters, they would have sensed him immediately.

Dashlegar cautiously crept through the cave entrance. He had put a spell on himself that would block his Dark Magic from being detected by the remaining Shifter. This worked because there was only one. He was sure five magic wielders would be able to pick up on his little trick, but he thought he could handle just one.

It was dark in the caves. Dashlegar thought about conjuring a light, but he wanted to surprise the lone Shifter and a ball of light wandering the caves would surely give him away. Instead, he used a minor spell that allowed him to sense the heat off the walls and floors. They would still be slightly warm from the other Shifters' departure.

As Dashlegar wound his way through the twisting stone walls, he found his spell didn't work perfectly. Several times the heat led him to a nest of Rathuuls, a raccoon-lizard hybrid species. He then had to back track and study the heat path more closely. Soon he sensed a greater heat. He dropped his spell and slowly moved along the wall. He saw the glow of a fire radiating off the wall opposite it.

"This must be where they stay, and where I'll find

the orb," Dashlegar said to himself.

He stood up, straightened his clothes and strode confidently around the corner. Melanthious jumped and unsheathed his sword.

"What are you doing here? We thought you were dead!"

"I'm here for the orb of course," Dashlegar said nonchalantly as he studied the tip of a stalagmite.

"That day by the forest Jerriney nearly killed you. A normal human would have died from that." Melanthious' face grew stern. "But you, you must have went to that Dark Mage and used *his* powers to heal you. You would not have been strong enough to do it on your own."

"True, I did use quite of bit of his magic to heal me. But you shouldn't be worrying about that now." Dashlegar looked at the Shifter and smirked. "You should be worrying about whether your death will be quick and painless, or long and terrifying."

Dashlegar swiftly pulled his rapier out and lunged at Melanthious. The Shifter quickly raised his blade and blocked the attack. "Even if you kill me, you won't be able to find the orb," he yelled at Dashlegar.

"Oh don't worry. I'll have no trouble killing you *and* finding the orb. Even if you've hidden it somewhere clever," Dashlegar calmly said as they danced around the fire, clanks of metal on metal echoing throughout the cave tunnels.

"How do you know if it's even here?" Melanthious questioned as he kicked ambers from the fire into Dashlegar. The man easily sidestepped the attempt.

"If it was with one of the others, there would be no need for you to be here guarding it. And, I know you did not stay behind because you wanted to. You looked so lonely when I snuck up on you." Dashlegar laughed at him.

"You fool!" Melanthious yelled. "You don't even know the extent of the orb's powers. If you use it, you will end up just like that Dark Mage, or worse. The orb is not some limitless magic holder. It is a portal to the demon realm." He dodged an attack from Dashlegar. "Hear me out Dashlegar! Put down your weapon!"

Dashlegar laughed again, swung his sword around his hand and stuck it in the ground. "Alright, you want to jabber on, I will grant the last wish of a man about to die."

"You do not know what you are dealing with. That orb needs to be destroyed. We cannot afford to have demons running around our world. They will take over and the human race will become extinct." Melanthious was almost pleading with him. He was not at his top strength so he hoped to talk Dashlegar out of pursuing this world-destroying orb.

Recently the Shifters noticed that the orb was starting to draw upon their magic, as if it was trying to open itself up. This was not a good sign so they began to search for older, wiser dragons and humans who might know how to destroy the orb safely. If they crushed it into pieces that would cause the portal to burst open with no way of closing it. This would also mean there would be no way of sending the demons back as they may only leave through the portal the entered.

"Demons you say?" Dashlegar raised an eyebrow as he casually grabbed his rapier. "They sound mighty powerful. Just think what I could accomplish with them on my side."

"They would not spare you. The moment you open the portal, they will kill you. Demons have no care for anyone, not even their own." Melanthious' strength was quickly waning. During the fight he had moved closer to the portal. It was pulling on his magic harder than ever. For this reason he could not use his powers against Dashlegar. The orb would take hold of it and use it for itself.

"Please Dashlegar, do not bring on the destruction of your own world."

Dashlegar noticed that Melanthious was becoming weak. He thought it quite odd since they had barely fought, but he would not pass up such a grand opportunity. He would have that orb and make slaves of the demons.

"Destruction of the human race," Dashlegar walked around Melanthious, keeping his rapier low, but ready. "Sounds a bit lonely."

Melanthious sighed a breath of relief and relaxed a bit. He thought his plan of talking Dashlegar out of seeking the orb had worked.

"But fun!" Dashlegar plunged his rapier into Melanthious' back, the blade going straight through his heart. He grabbed the dying Shifter and whispered into his ear, "Sorry you won't be there to see it."

Dashlegar jerked the blade from Melanthious. As the Shifter fell, a wisp-like substance slowly came out of him. Dashlegar watched as it moved around him and deeper into the room.

He followed the tendril to a dark corner. The wispy cloud went into a pile of rocks. Dashlegar threw his sword on the ground and fell to his knees, quickly tearing the pile apart. Under the rocks was a chest with chains around it. He could tell they were magical chains, meant to kill those who opened it with the wrong key. He had seen many of these in his travels, they were popular among smugglers and treasure seekers who wanted to keep their most valued wares secure. Dashlegar knew a man who specialized in opening such chests.

Using his Dark Magic, he quickly checked around the small container to see if there were any traps that would be set off upon lifting the chest. There were none.

Dashlegar chuckled. "How foolish," he said to himself. He released the spell. As his did, he noticed it drained him more than it should have. He waved the feeling off to being already tired from the fight. Dashlegar picked up the chained chest and hurried out of the cave system, not wanting to encounter any of the other Shifters.

Thank You

I would like to say thank you, first off, to my mother who introduced me to my publisher and basically got this whole thing started. Both my parents, as well as my grandmother, are very supportive and put plenty time and money into creating this book. Much thanks to my publisher, Linda L. Young, who saw great potential in me and took me on in abnormal circumstances, and to others involved with MaxQ Enterprises who helped as well. Your time and effort, and faith in me, are much appreciated.

Thanks to friends and family for encouraging and supporting me and prompting me to write more books (which there will be). A special thanks goes to my best friend, Robyn Krause. When I started writing this book in Junior High we worked on it a little bit together. She helped create Ron and Liz's house and Jerriney as a child. She also taught me how to be more descriptive in my scenes.

And finally, thanks to all who purchase this book and those to come. Writing and creating fantasy worlds is something I enjoy a lot. It's exciting to hear that other people enjoy it as well.

298

Find other great books at:

www.maxqenterprises.com

The Waiting Cross

Forest of Fears

Turf Tales

Sports Broadcaster's Handbook

Heeere's Dusty

Whisper Upon The Wind

End Of The Rope

Annie's Ordeal

Moving To Maui Guide

C61

What's That Smell?